A Book of Old English Fairy Tales

Fairy Gold

CHOSEN BY ERNEST RHYS

ILLUSTRATED BY HERBERT COLE

DOVER PUBLICATIONS, INC.
MINEOLA, NEW YORK

Bibliographical Note

This Dover edition, first published in 2008, is a republication of Part I of the work originally published by J. M. Dent & Sons Ltd., London, and E.P. Dutton & Co., New York, in 1906. Seven color plates scattered throughout Part I of the original edition appear after page 122.

DOVER *Pictorial Archive* SERIES

This book belongs to the Dover Pictorial Archive Series. You may use the designs and illustrations for graphics and crafts applications, free and without special permission, provided that you include no more than four in the same publication or project. (For permission for additional use, please write to Permissions Department, Dover Publications, Inc., 31 East 2nd Street, Mineola, N.Y. 11501.)

However, republication or reproduction of any illustration by any other graphic service, whether it be in a book or in any other design resource, is strictly prohibited.

International Standard Book Number

ISBN-13: 978-0-486-46138-0
ISBN-10: 0-486-46138-6

Manufactured in the United States of America
Dover Publications, Inc., 31 East 2nd Street, Mineola, N.Y. 11501

OBERON KING OF FAYS

FAIRY-GOLD

FAIRY TALES and ROMANCES

CONTENTS

A Book of Old English Fairy Tales

FAIRY GOLD

♧ THE IMP TREE ♧

NCE there was a King of Winchester called Orfeo, and dearly he loved his queen, Heurodis. She happened one hot afternoon in summer-time to be walking in the orchard, when she became very drowsy; and she lay down under an imp tree,[1] and there she fell fast asleep. While she slept, she had a strange dream. She

[1] The "Imp Tree" is not as you might suppose, a tree of the imps, but a tree on which a branch of another tree has been "imped" or grafted.

3

dreamt that two fair knights came to her side, and bade her come quickly with them to speak to their lord and king. But she answered them right boldly, that she neither dared nor cared to go with them. So the two knights went away; but very quickly they returned, bringing their king with them, and a thousand knights in his train, and many beauteous ladies drest in pure white, riding on snow-white steeds. The king had a crown on his head, not of silver or red-gold, but all of precious stones that shone like the sun. By his side was led a lady's white palfrey that seemed to be prepared for some rider, for its saddle was empty. He commanded that Heurodis should be placed upon this white steed, and thereupon the King of Faërie and his train of knights and white dames, and Heurodis beside him, rode off through a fair country with many flowery meads, fields, forests and pleasant waters, where stood castles and towers amid the green trees. Fairest of all, on a green terrace overlooking many orchards and rose-gardens, stood the Faërie King's palace. When he had shown these things to Heurodis, he brought her back safe to the Imp Tree; but he bade her, on pain of death, meet him under the same tree on the morrow.

When Heurodis awoke from this dream, it was to find Orfeo standing at her side. She told him of all that had happened ; of the Faërie King and of the green faërie country she had visited. He resolved that on the morrow he and a thousand knights should stand

When Heurodis awoke from this dream, it was to find Orfeo
standing at her side.

armed round the Imp Tree to protect her from the
Faërie King. And when the time came, there they
stood like a ring of living steel or a hedge of spears,
to guard Heurodis. But in spite of all, she was snatched
away under their very eyes; and in vain were all their
efforts to see which way she and her faërie captors were
gone.

Orfeo made search for his lost queen everywhere

during many days, but no footstep of her was to be found in upper earth. And then in sorrow for her, and in utter despair, he left his palace at Winchester, gave up his throne and went into the wilderness, carrying only a harp for companion. With its tunes, as he sang to it, sorrowing for Heurodis, the wild beasts were enchanted and often came round about him—yea, wolf and fox, bear and little squirrel—to hear him play. And there in the forest, Orfeo (as the old story-book says) :

> " Often in hot undertides [1]
> Would see the Faërie King besides,
> The King of Faërie with his rout
> Hunt and ride all roundabout,
> With calls and elfin-horns that blew,
> And hounds that did reply thereto,
> But never pulled down hart or doe,
> And never arrow left the bow."

And sometimes he saw the Faërie Host pass, as if to war, the knights with their swords drawn, stout and fierce of face, and their banners flying. Other times he saw these faërie knights and ladies dance, dressed like guisers, with tabors beating and joyous trumpets blowing. And one day Orfeo saw sixty lovely ladies ride out to the riverside for falconry, each with her falcon on her bare hand, and in the very midst of them (oh wonder !) rode his lost queen, Heurodis. He determined at once to follow them ; and after flying their falcons they return through the forest at evening to a wild rocky place, where they ride into the rock through a rude cleft,

[1] Afternoons.

HERBERT COLE. 06

Orfeo went into the wilderness carrying only a harp for companion ~

overhung with brambles. They ride in, a league and more, till they come to the fairest country ever seen, where it is high midsummer and broad sunlight. In its midst stands a palace of an hundred towers, with walls of crystal, and windows coped and arched with gold. All that land was light, because when the night should come, the precious stones in the palace walls gave out a light as bright as noonday. Into this palace hall Orfeo entered, in the train of the ladies, and saw there the King of Faërie on his throne. The king was enraged at first when he saw the strange man enter with his harp. But Orfeo offers to play upon it, and Heurodis, when she hears, is filled with longing, while the Faërie King is so enchanted that he promises to Orfeo any gift he likes to ask out of all the riches of the faërie regions. But Orfeo, to this, has only one word to reply :—

"HEURODIS !"

And the King of Faërie thereupon gives her back to Orfeo, and they return in great joy, hand in hand together, through the wilderness to Winchester, where they live and reign together for ever afterwards in peace and happiness. But let none who would not be carried away like Heurodis to the Faërie King's country dare to sleep in the undertide beneath the Imp Tree.

THE PIXY FLOWER

NCE upon a time there lived in Devonshire two serving damsels, called Molly and Sabina, who were very fond of ribands and finery. When their mistress scolded them for spending more money than they ought upon such things, they said the pixies were very kind to them, and would often drop silver for their pleasure into a bucket of fair water which they placed for the accommodation of those little beings in the chimney corner every night before they went to bed. Once, however, it was forgotten, and the pixies, finding themselves disappointed by an empty bucket, whisked upstairs to the maids' bedroom, popped through the keyhole, and began to exclaim aloud against the laziness and neglect of the damsels. Now Sabina, who lay awake and heard all this, jogged her fellow-servant, and proposed getting up immediately to put things straight. But Molly, lazy girl, who liked not being disturbed out of a comfortable nap, pettishly declared " that, for her part, she would not stir out of bed to please all the pixies in Devonshire." The good-humoured Sabina, however, got up, filled the bucket, and was rewarded

He insisted upon striking Molly with it on the lame leg.

by a handful of silver pennies found in it the next morning. But long ere that time had arrived, what was her alarm, as she crept towards the bed, to hear all the elves buzzing like so many angry bees, and consulting as to what should be done to the lazy, lazy lass who would not stir out of bed for their pleasure.

Some proposed "pinches, nips, and bobs," others wanted to spoil her new cherry-coloured bonnet and ribands. One talked of sending her the toothache, another of giving her a red nose ; but this last was voted much too bad a punishment for a pretty young lass. So, tempering mercy with justice, the pixies were kind enough to let her off with a lame leg, which was to plague her for seven years, and was only to be cured by a certain herb, growing on Dartmoor. Its long, and learned, and very queer and difficult name the elfin judge pronounced in a high and shrill voice. It was a name of seven syllables, seven being also the number of years decreed for Molly's lameness.

Sabina, good-natured maid, wishing to save her fellow-damsel so long a suffering, tried with might and main to bear in mind the name of this strange herb. She said it over and over again, tied a knot in her garter at every syllable as a help to memory, and thought she had the word just as safe and sure as her own name, and very possibly felt much more anxious about retaining the one than the other.

At length she dropped asleep, and did not wake till the morning. Now whether Sabina's head was like a sieve, that lets out as fast as it takes in, or if the over-exertion to remember only caused her to forget, cannot be determined ; but certain it is that when she opened her eyes she knew nothing at all about the matter, excepting that Molly was to go lame on her right leg for seven long years, unless a herb with a strange name could be got to cure her. And lame Molly went for nearly the whole of those seven years.

At length, about the end of that time, Sabina and Molly went out into the fields early one morning to pick mushrooms, when a merry, squint-eyed, queer-looking boy started up all of a sudden just as Molly went to pluck a fine big one and came tumbling, head over heels, towards her. He held in his hand a green herb with a tiny yellow flower, which some say was called *Inula-Helenium*[1] and he insisted upon striking Molly with it on the lame leg. From that very moment she got well, and lame Molly became the best dancer in the whole town when she and Sabina danced at the feast of Mayday on the green.

[1] Ploughman's Spikenard : Elecampane.

Ploughman's Spikenard

HERBERT COLE '06

THE BLACK BULL OF NORROWAY

> To wilder measures next they turn :
>   The black, black bull of Norroway !
> Sudden the tapers cease to burn,
>   The minstrels cease to play !

ONCE upon a time there lived a king who had three daughters ; the two eldest were proud and ugly, but the youngest was the gentlest and most beautiful creature ever seen, and the pride not only of her father and mother, but of all in the land. As it fell out, the three princesses were talking one night of whom they would marry. "I will have no one lower

15

than a king," said the eldest princess. The second
would take a prince or a great duke even. "Pho,
pho," said the youngest, laughing, "you are both so
proud ; now, I would be content with the Black Bull
o' Norroway." Well, they thought no more of the
matter till the next morning, when, as they sat at
breakfast, they heard the most dreadful bellowing at
the door, and what should it be but the Black Bull
come for his bride. You may be sure they were all
terribly frightened at this, for the Black Bull was one
of the most horrible creatures ever seen in the world.
And the king and queen did not know how to save
their daughter. At last they determined to send him
off with the old henwife. So they put her on his back,
and away he went with her till he came to a great
black forest, when, throwing her down, he returned,
roaring louder and more frightfully than ever. They
then sent, one by one, all the servants, then the two
eldest princesses ; but not one of them met with any
better treatment than the old henwife, and at last they
were forced to send their youngest and favourite
child.

Far she travelled upon the Black Bull, through
many dreadful forests and lonely wastes, till they came
at last to a noble castle, where a large company was
assembled. The lord of the castle pressed them to
stay, though much he wondered at the lovely princess
and her strange companion. But as they went in
among the guests, the princess espied a pin sticking

in the Black Bull's hide, which she pulled out, and, to the surprise of all, there appeared not a frightful wild beast, but one of the most beautiful princes ever beheld.

You may believe how delighted the princess was to see him fall at her feet, and thank her for breaking his cruel enchantment. There were great rejoicings in the castle at this, but alas ! in the midst of them he suddenly disappeared, and though every place was sought, he was nowhere to be found.

The princess, from being filled with happiness, was all but broken-hearted. She determined, however, to seek through all the world for him, and many weary ways she went, but for a long, long while nothing could she hear of her lover. Travelling once through a dark wood, she lost her way, and as night was coming on, she thought she must now certainly die of cold and hunger ; but seeing a light through the trees, she went on till she came to a little hut, where an old woman lived, who took her in, and gave her both food and shelter. In the morning the old wifie gave her three nuts, that she was not to break till her heart was "like to break and owre again like to break "; so, showing her the way, she bade God speed her, and the princess once more set out on her wearisome journey.

She had not gone far till a company of lords and ladies rode past her, all talking merrily of the fine doings they expected at the Duke o' Norroway's wedding. Then she came up to a number of people carrying all sorts of fine things, and they, too, were going to the duke's wedding. At last she came to a castle, where nothing was to be seen but cooks and bakers, some running one way, and some another, and all so busy that they did not know what to do first. Whilst she was looking at all this, she heard a noise of hunters behind her, and some one cried out,—

"Make way for the Duke o' Norroway!"

And who should ride past but the prince and a beautiful lady.

You may be sure her heart was now "like to break and owre again like to break" at this sad sight, so she broke one of the nuts, and out came a wee wifie carding wool. The princess then went into the castle, and asked to see the lady, who no sooner saw the wee wifie so hard at work, than she offered the princess anything in her castle for it.

"I will give it to you," said she, "only on condition that you put off for one day your marriage with the Duke o' Norroway, and that I may go into his room alone to-night."

So anxious was the lady for the nut, that she consented. And when dark night was come, and the duke fast asleep, the princess was put alone into his chamber. Sitting down by his bedside, she began singing :—

"Far hae I sought ye, near am I brought to ye,
    Dear Duke o' Norroway, will ye no turn and speak
    to me?"

 You may be sure her heart was now "like to break, and owre again like to break"~

HERBERT COLE · 1906.

Though she sang this over and over again, the duke never wakened, and in the morning the princess had to leave him, without his knowing she had ever been there. She then broke the second nut, and out came a wee wifie spinning, which so delighted the lady, that she readily agreed to put off her marriage another day for it; but the princess came no better speed the second night than the first, and, almost in depair, she broke the last nut, which contained a wee wifie reeling, and on the same condition as before, the lady got possession of it.

When the duke was dressing in the morning, his man asked him what the strange singing and moaning that had been heard in his room for two nights meant.

" I heard nothing," said the duke ; " it could only have been your fancy."

" Take no sleeping-draught to-night, and be sure to lay aside your pillow of heaviness," said the man, " and you also will hear what for two nights has kept me awake."

The duke did so, and the princess coming in, sat down sighing at his bedside, thinking this the last time she might ever see him. The duke started up when he heard the voice of his dearly-loved princess ; and with many endearing expressions of surprise and joy, explained to her that he had long been in the power of a witch-wife, whose spells over him were now happily ended by their once again meeting.

The princess, happy to be the means of breaking

his second evil spell, consented to marry him, and the wicked witch-wife, who fled that country, afraid of the duke's anger, has never since been heard of. All was hurry and preparation in the castle, and the marriage which took place happily ended the adventures of the Black Bull o' Norroway, and the wanderings of the king's daughter.

R. C.

⁑ THE LAMBTON WORM ⁑

LONG, long ago,—I cannot say how long,—the
young heir of Lambton Castle led a careless,
profane life, regardless of God and man. All his
Saturday nights he spent in drinking, and all his
Sunday mornings in fishing. One Sunday, he had cast
his line into the Water of Wear many times without a
bite; and at last in a rage he let loose his tongue in
curses loud and deep, to the great scandal of the
servants and country-folk as they passed by to the old
chapel at Brugeford, which was not in ruins then.

Soon afterwards he felt something tugging at his line, and trusting he had at last hooked a fine fish, he used all his skill to play it and bring it safe to land. But what were his horror and dismay on finding that, instead of a fish he had only caught a loathly worm of most evil appearance! He hastily tore the foul thing from his hook, and flung it into a well close by, which is still known by the name of the Worm Well.

The young heir had scarcely thrown his line again into the stream when a stranger of venerable appearance, passing by, asked him what sport he had met with?

He replied : "Why, truly, I think I have caught the evil one himself. Look in and judge."

The stranger looked, and remarked that he had never seen the like of it before ; that it resembled an eft, only it had nine holes on each side of its mouth ; and, finally, that he thought it boded no good.

The worm remained there unheeded in the well till it outgrew so confined a dwelling-place. It then emerged, and betook itself by day to the river, where it lay coiled round a rock in the middle of the stream, and by night to a neighbouring hill, round whose base it would twine itself, while it continued to grow so fast that it soon could encircle the hill three times. This eminence is still called the Worm Hill. It is oval in shape, on the north side of the Wear, and about a mile and a half from old Lambton Hall.

The Lambton Worm now became the terror of the whole country side. It sucked the cows' milk, worried the cattle, devoured the lambs, and committed every sort of depredation on the helpless peasantry. Having laid waste the district on the north side of the river, it crossed the stream and approached Lambton Hall, where the old lord was living alone and desolate. His son had repented of his evil life, and had gone to the wars in a distant country. Some people say he had gone as a crusader to the Holy Land.

On hearing of the dreaded Worm's approach, the terrified household assembled in council. Much was said, but to little purpose, till the steward, a man of age and experience, advised that the large trough which stood in the courtyard should immediately be filled with milk. This was done without delay ; the monster approached, drank the milk, and, without doing further harm, returned across the Wear to wrap his giant form around his favourite hill. The next day he was seen recrossing the river ; the trough was hastily filled again, and with the same results. It was found that the milk of " nine kye " was needed to fill the trough ; and if this quantity was not placed there everyday, regularly and in full measure, the Worm would break out into a violent rage, lashing its tail round the trees in the park, and tearing them up by the roots.

The Lambton Worm was now, in fact, the terror of the whole country. Many a knight had come out to fight with it, but all to no purpose ; for it possessed the marvellous power of reuniting itself after being cut asunder, and thus was more than a match for all the knighthood of the North. So, after many a vain conflict, and the loss of many a brave man, the creature was left in possession of its favourite hill.

After seven long years, however, the heir of Lambton returned home, to find the broad lands of his ancestors waste and desolate, his people terror-stricken or in hiding, his father sinking into the grave overwhelmed with care and anxiety. He took no rest, we are told, till he had crossed the river and surveyed the Worm as it lay coiled round the foot of the Worm Hill; then, hearing how every other knight and man-at-arms had failed, he took counsel in the matter from the Wise-woman of Chester-le-Street.

At first the Wise-woman of Chester-le-Street did nothing but upbraid him for having brought this scourge upon his house and neighbourhood; but when she saw that he was indeed penitent, and eager at any cost to remove the evil he had caused, she bade him get his best suit of mail studded thickly with spear-heads, to put it on, and thus armed to take his stand on the rock in the middle of the river Wear. There he must meet the Worm face to face, trusting the issue to Providence and his good sword. But she charged him before going to the encounter to take a vow, that, if successful, he would slay the first living thing that met him on his way homewards. Should he fail to fulfil this vow, she warned him that for nine generations no lord of Lambton would die in his bed.

The heir, now a belted knight, made the vow in

He struck a violent blow upon the monster's head as it passed.

Brugeford Chapel. He studded his armour back and
breast-plate, greaves and armlets, with the sharpest
spear-heads, and unsheathing his trusty sword took his
stand on the rock in the middle of the Wear. At
the accustomed hour the Worm uncoiled its "snaky
twine," and wound its way towards the hall, crossing
the river close by the rock on which the knight was
standing eager for the combat. He struck a violent
blow upon the monster's head as it passed, on which
the creature turned on him, and writhing and lashing
the water in its rage, flung its tail round him, as if to
strangle him in its coils.[1]

But the closer the Worm wrapped him in its folds
the more deadly were its self-inflicted wounds, till at last

---

[1] There is a modern ballad, which describes the death-grapple
of the Worm :—

> "The Worm shot down the middle stream
> Like a flash of living light,
> And the waters kindled round his path
> In rainbow colours bright.
>
> But when he saw the armed knight
> He gathered all his pride,
> And, coiled in many a radiant spire,
> Rode buoyant o'er the tide.
>
> When he darted at length his dragon strength
> An earthquake shook the rock ;
> The fireflakes bright fell round the knight
> But unmoved he met the shock.
>
> Though his heart was stout it quailed no doubt,
> His very life-blood ran cold,
> As round and round the wild Worm wound
> In many a grappling fold."

the river ran crimson with its blood. As its strength diminished, the knight redoubled his strokes, and he was able at last with his good sword to cut the serpent fold by fold, and piece by piece asunder ; each severed part was immediately borne away by the swiftness of the current, and the Worm, unable to reunite itself, was utterly destroyed.

During this long and terrible combat in the river, the household of Lambton had shut themselves within-doors to pray for their young lord, he having promised that when it was over he would, if conqueror, blow a blast on his bugle. This would assure his father of his safety, and warn them to let loose a favourite hound, which they had destined as the victim, according to the Wise-woman's word and the young lord's vow. When, however, the bugle-notes were heard within the hall, the old lord of Lambton forgot everything but his son's safety, and rushing out of doors, ran to meet and embrace him.

The heir of Lambton felt his heart turn sick as he saw his old father come. What could he do? He could not lift his hand against his beloved father ; yet how else could he fulfil his vow? In his perplexity he blew another blast ; the hound was let loose, it bounded to its master ; the sword, yet reeking with the Lambton Worm's blood, was plunged into its heart. But it was all in vain. The vow was broken. What the Wise-woman of Chester-le-Street had foretold came true. The curse lay upon the house of Lambton for nine generations.

In two months but a day, the King
Has brought his new Queen home ~

The Laidley Worm of Spindleston [1]

I

THE king has sailed from Bambrough sands,
    Long may May Margaret mourn!
Long may she stand on the castle wall,
    Looking for his return.

She has counted the keys of each chamber ;
    And knotted them on a string.
She has cast them o'er her left shoulder,
    To bring good-luck to the king.

She trippéd out, she trippéd in,
    She tript into the yard ;
But it was more for the old king's sake,
    Than for the new queen's regard.

---

[1] Worm was an old word for a serpent, and "laidley" means loathly, or horrible.

33

II

In two months but a day, the king
  Has brought his new queen home ;
And all the lords in the north country,
  To welcome them are come.

" And welcome, father ! " says May Margaret :
  " Unto your halls and bowers !
And welcome too, my step-mother,
  For all that's here is yours ! "

A Scots lord said, that heard her speak :
  " This Lady Margaret's grace
Surpasseth all of womankind,
  She has so fair a face ! "

With that the new queen turned about :—
  " You might have excepted me ;
But I will bring May Margaret down
  To a Laidley Worm's degree.

I will bring her low as a Laidley Worm,
  That warps ¹ about the stone ;
And not, till the Childe of Wynde comes back,
  Shall her witching be undone ! "

The princess stood at the bower door
  Laughing,—and who could blame ?
But e'er the next day's sun went down,
  A long worm she became.

              ¹ Wraps itself.

For seven miles east, and seven miles west,
 And seven miles north and south,
No blade of grass or corn could grow,
 So fiery was her mouth.

The milk of seven white milch-kine,
 Was brought her at morning light ;
The milk of seven white milch-kine,
 She drank at fall of night.

Word went east, and word went west,
 And word went over the sea,
That a Laidley Worm in Spindleston Heughs,
 Would ruin the North Country.

Word went east, and word went west,
 Word went across the sea ;
The Childe of Wynde got wit of it,
 And it fretted him wondrously.

He called about him his men-at-arms,
 " To Bambrough we must sail :—
And we must land by Spindleston,
 This Laidley Worm to quell."

They built a ship without delay,
 With masts of the rowan tree,
With fluttering sails of silk and hemp,
 And set her on the sea.

Next morn the wicked queen looked out.

III

NEXT morn the wicked queen looked out,
  To see what could be seen :
There she espied a gallant ship,
  Before the castle green.

When she beheld the silken sails,
  Full glancing in the sun,
To sink the ship she sent away
  Her witch-wives, every one.

In vain, in vain!   The witch-wives came
  Back where the witch-queen stood—
For know that witches have no power,
  Where there is rowan-tree wood.

O, then the queen sent the Laidley Worm,
  To make the top-masts heel,—
And the Laidley Worm has wormed the sand,
  And crept beneath the keel.

The worm leapt up, the worm leapt down,
  And plaited around each plank ;
And aye as the ship came near the quay,
  She heeled till she nearly sank.

But the Childe of Wynde he put about,
  And he steered for Budley-sand ;
And jumping into the shallow sea,
  He is safely got to land.

And there he drew his sword of proof,
  For the worm was close behind ;
But ere he struck he heard a voice,
  So soft as summer-wind :

" Oh ! quit thy sword, unbend thy bow,
  And give me kisses three ;
For though I seem a Laidley Worm
  No hurt I'll do to thee!

Oh ! quit thy sword, unbend thy bow,
　　And give me kisses three ;
If I'm not won ere set of sun,
　　Won I shall never be."

He quitted his sword, and kissed her thrice,
　　The wet sand at his feet ;
She sank in the sand a Laidley Worm,—
　　She rose up May Margaret.

She trembled in the cold sea-air,
　　But his mantle has wrapt her round,
And they are up to Bambrough Castle,
　　As fast as horn can sound.

The witch-queen stood upon the stair,
　　Twisting her wicked hands :
" Oh ! who is this ? " said the Childe of Wynde,
　　" That on the stairway stands ? "

" Woe, woe to thee, thou wicked witch,
　　An ill death mayest thou die ;
The doom thou dreed on May Margaret,
　　The same doom shalt thou dree.

I will turn you into a Laidley Toad,
　　That still in the clay doth wend ;
And won, won, shalt thou never be !
　　Till this world hath an end !"

HERBERT COLE 1906

She trembled in the cold sea-air,
But his mantle has wrapt her round.

THE GREEN KNIGHT

I

WHEN Arthur was King of Britain, and so reigned, it befell one winter-tide he held at Camelot his Christmas feast, with all the knights of the Round Table, full fifteen days. All was joy then in hall and chamber; and when the New Year came, it was kept with great joy. Rich gifts were given and many lords and ladies took their seats at the table, where Queen Guenever sat at the king's side, and a lady fairer of form might no one say he had ever before seen. But King Arthur would not eat nor would he long sit, until he should have witnessed some wondrous adventure. The first course was served with a blowing of trumpets, and before each two guests were set twelve dishes, and bright wine, for there was no want of anything.

Scarcely had the first course commenced, when there rushed in at the hall-door a knight,—the tallest on earth he must have been. His back and breast were broad, but his waist was small. He was clothed

entirely in green, and his spurs were of bright gold;
his saddle was embroidered with birds and flies, and
the steed that he rode upon was green. Gaily was the
knight attired ; his great beard, like a green bush, hung
on his breast. His horse's mane was decked with
golden threads, and its tail bound with a green band;
such a horse and such a knight were never before seen.
It seemed that no man might endure the Green
Knight's blows, but he carried neither spear nor shield.
In one hand he held a holly bough, and in the other an
axe the edge of which was as keen as a sharp razor,
and the handle was encased in iron, curiously graven
with green.

Thus arrayed, the Green Knight entered the hall,
without saluting anyone ; and asked for the governor
of the company, and looked about him for the most
renowned of them. Much they marvelled to see a
man and a horse as green as grass ; never before had
they seen such a sight as this ; they were afraid to
answer, and were as silent as if sleep had taken hold of
them, some from fear, others from courtesy. King
Arthur, who was never afraid, saluted the Green
Knight, and bade him welcome. The Green Knight
said that he would not tarry ; he was seeking the most
valiant, that he might prove him. He came in peace ;
but he had a halberd at home and a helmet too. King
Arthur assured him that he should not fail to find an
opponent worthy of him.

"I seek no fight," said the knight; "here are

only beardless children; here is no man to match me; still, if any be bold enough to strike a stroke for another, this axe shall be his, but I shall give him a stroke in return within a twelvemonth and a day!"

Fear kept all silent; while the knight rolled his red eyes about and bent his gristly green brows. Waving his beard awhile, he exclaimed,—

"What, then—is this Arthur's Court? Forsooth, the renown of the Round Table is overturned with a word of one man's speech!"

Arthur grew red for shame, and waxed as wroth as the wind. He assured the knight that no one was afraid of his great words, and seized the axe. The Green Knight, stroking his beard, awaited the blow, and with a dry countenance drew down his green coat.

But thereupon Sir Gawayne begged the king to let him undertake the blow; he asked permission to leave the table, saying it was not meet that Arthur should take the game, while so many bold knights sat upon bench. Although the weakest, he was quite ready to meet the Green Knight. The other knights too begged Arthur to "give Gawayne the game." Then the king gave Gawayne, who was his nephew, his weapon and told him to keep heart and hand steady. The Green Knight inquired the name of his opponent, and Sir Gawayne told him his name, declaring that he was willing to give and receive a blow.

"It pleases me well, Sir Gawayne," says the Green

Knight, "that I shall receive a blow from thy fist ; but thou must swear that thou wilt seek me to receive the blow in return."

"Where shall I seek thee ?" says Sir Gawayne ; "tell me thy name and thy abode and I will find thee."

"When thou hast smitten me," says the Green Knight, "then tell I thee of my home and name ; if I speak not at all, so much the better for thee. Take now thy grim weapon and let us see how thou strikest ?"

"Gladly, sir, forsooth," quoth Sir Gawayne.

And now the Green Knight puts his long, green locks aside, and lays bare his neck, and Sir Gawayne strikes hard with the axe, and at one blow severs the head from the body. The head falls to the earth, and many treat it roughly, but the Green Knight never falters ; he starts up, seizes his head, steps into the saddle, holding the while the head in his hand by the hair, and turns his horse about. Then lo ! the head lifts up its eyelids, and addresses Sir Gawayne :—

"Look thou, be ready to go as thou hast promised, and seek till thou findest me. Get thee to the Green Chapel, there to receive a blow on New Year's morn ; fail thou never ; come, or recreant be called." So saying, the Green Knight rides out of the hall, his head in his hand.

And now Arthur addresses the queen : "Dear dame, be not dismayed ; such marvels well become the Christmas festival ; I may now go to meat. Sir Gawayne, hang up thine axe." The king and his knights sit feasting at the board, with all manner of meat and minstrelsy, till day is ended.

"But beware, Sir Gawayne!" said the king at its end, "lest thou fail to seek the adventure which thou hast taken in hand!"

II

LIKE other years, the months and seasons of this year pass away full quickly and never return. After Christmas comes Lent, and spring sets in, and warm showers descend. Then the groves become green; and birds build and sing for joy of the summer that follows; blossoms begin to bloom, and noble notes are heard in the woods. With the soft winds of summer, more beautiful grow the flowers, wet with dew-drops. But then harvest approaches, and drives the dust about, and the leaves drop off the trees, the grass becomes grey, and all ripens and rots. At last, when the winter winds come round again, Sir Gawayne thinks of his dread journey and his vow to the Green Knight.

On All-Hallow's Day, Arthur makes a feast for his nephew's sake. After meat, Sir Gawayne thus speaks to his uncle: "Now, liege lord, I ask leave of you, for I am bound on the morrow to seek the Green Knight.'

Many noble knights, the best of the Court, counsel and comfort him, and much sorrow prevails in the hall, but Gawayne declares that he has nothing to fear.

On the morn he asks for his arms; a carpet is spread
on the floor, and he steps thereon. He is dubbed in
a doublet of Tarsic silk, and a well-made hood; they
set steel shoes on his feet, lap his legs in steel greaves;
put on the steel habergeon, the well-burnished braces,
elbow pieces, and gloves of plate: while over all is
placed the coat armour. His spurs are then fixed, and
his sword is attached to his side by a silken girdle.
Thus attired the knight hears mass, and afterwards
takes leave of Arthur and his Court. By that time
his horse Gringolet was ready, the harness of which
glittered like the gleam of the sun. Then Sir Gawayne
sets his helmet upon his head, and the circle around it
was decked with diamonds; and they give him his
shield with the " pentangle " of pure gold, devised by
King Solomon as a token of truth; for it is called the
endless knot, and well becomes the good Sir Gawayne,
a knight the truest of speech and the fairest of form.
He was found faultless in his five wits; the image of
the Virgin was depicted upon his shield; in courtesy
he was never found wanting, and therefore was the
endless knot fastened on his shield.

And now Sir Gawayne seizes his lance and bids all
" Good-day "; he spurs his horse and goes on his way.
All that saw him go, mourned in their hearts, and
declared that his equal was not to be found upon earth.
It would have been better for him to have been a leader
of men, than to die by the hands of an elvish man.

Meanwhile, many a weary mile goes Sir Gawayne;

now rides the knight through the realms of England; he has no companion but his horse, and no men does he see till he approaches North Wales. From Holyhead he passes into Wirral, where he finds but few that love God or man; he inquires after the Green Knight of the Green Chapel, but can gain no tidings of him. His cheer oft changed before he found the chapel; many a cliff he climbed over, many a ford and stream he crossed, and everywhere he found a foe. It were too tedious to tell the tenth part of his adventures with serpents, wolves and wild men; with bulls, bears and boars. Had he not been both brave and good, doubtless he had been dead; the sharp winter was far worse than any war that ever troubled him. Thus in peril he travels till Christmas Eve and on the morn he finds himself in a deep forest, where were old oaks many a hundred; and many sad birds upon bare twigs piped piteously for the cold. Through rough ways and deep mire he goes, that he may celebrate the birth of Christ and blessing himself he says, "Cross of Christ, speed me!"

Scarcely had he blessed himself thrice, than he saw a dwelling in the wood, set on a hill, the comeliest castle that knight ever owned, which shone as the sun through the bright oaks.

Forthwith Sir Gawayne goes to the chief gate, and finds the drawbridge raised, and the gates fast shut; as he abides there on the bank, he observes the high walls of hard hewn stone, with battlements and towers

and chalk-white chimneys ; and bright and great were
its round towers with their well-made capitals. Oh,
thinks he, if only he might come within the cloister.
Anon he calls, and soon there comes a porter to know
the knight's errand.

"Good sir," says Gawayne, "ask the high lord of
this house to grant me a lodging."

"You are welcome to dwell here as long as you
like," replied the porter. Thereupon is the drawbridge
let down, and the gate opened wide to receive him ;
and he enters and his horse is well stabled, and knights
and squires bring Gawayne into the hall. Many a one
hastens to take his helmet and sword ; the lord of the
castle bids him welcome and they embrace each other.
Gawayne looks on his host ; a big bold one he seemed ;
beaver-hued was his broad beard, and his face as fell as
the fire.

The lord then leads Gawayne to a chamber, and
assigns a page to wait upon him. In this bright bower
was noble bedding ; the curtains were of pure silk with
golden hems, and Tarsic tapestries covered the walls
and floor. Here the knight doffed his armour, and put
on rich robes, which well became him : and in troth a
more comely knight than Sir Gawayne was never seen.

Then a chair was placed by the fireplace for him,
and a mantle of fine linen, richly embroidered, thrown
over him ; a table, too, was brought in, and the
knight, having washed, was invited to sit to meat. He
was served with numerous dishes, with fish baked

and broiled, or boiled and seasoned with spices; full noble feast, and much mirth did he make, as he ate and drank.

Then Sir Gawayne, in answer to his host, told him he was of Arthur's Court; and when this was made known, great was the joy in the hall. Each one said softly to his mate: "Now we shall see courteous manners and hear noble speech, for we have amongst us the father of all nurture."

After dinner, the company go to the chapel, to hear the evensong of the great season. The lord of the castle and Sir Gawayne sit together during the service. When his wife, accompanied by her maids, left her seat after the service, she appeared even fairer than Guenever. An older dame led her by the hand, and very unlike they were; for if the young one was fair, the other was yellow, and had rough and wrinkled cheeks. The younger had a throat fairer than snow; the elder had black brows and bleared lips. With permission of the lord, Sir Gawayne salutes the elder, and the younger courteously kisses, and begs to be her servant. To the great hall then they go, where spices and wine are served: the lord takes off his hood, and places it on a spear: he who makes most mirth that Christmastide is to win it.

On Christmas morn, joy reigns in every dwelling in the world; so did it in the castle where Sir Gawayne now abode. The lord and the old ancient wife sit together, and Sir Gawayne sits by the wife of his host;

it were too tedious to tell of the meat, the mirth, and
the joy that abounded everywhere. Trumpets and
horns give forth their merry notes, and great was the
joy for three days.

St. John's Day was the last day of the Christmas
festival, and on the morrow many of the guests took
their departure from the castle. Its lord thanked Sir
Gawayne for the honour and pleasure of his visit, and
endeavoured to keep him at his court. He desired also
to know what had driven Sir Gawayne from Arthur's
Court before the end of the Christmas holidays?

Sir Gawayne replied that " a high errand and a hasty
one " had forced him to leave the Court. Then he asked
his host whether he had ever heard of the Green
Chapel? For there he had to be on New Year's Day,
and he would as lief die as fail in his errand. The
prince tells Sir Gawayne he will teach him the way, and
that the Green Chapel is not more than two miles from
the castle. Then was Gawayne glad, and he consented
to tarry awhile at the castle ; and its lord and castellan
rejoiced too, and sent to ask the ladies to come and
entertain their guest. And he asked Sir Gawayne to
grant him one request : that he would keep his chamber
on the morrow's morn, as he must be tired after his
far travel. Meanwhile his host and the other men of
the castle were to rise very early, and go a-hunting.

" Whatsoever," said his host, " I win in the wood
shall be yours ; and whatever hap be yours at home, I
will as freely count as mine." And he gave Sir

Gawayne in token a ring, which he was not to yield,
no, not though it was thrice required of him by the
fairest lady under heaven ! To all this Sir Gawayne
gladly agreed, and so with much cheer, a bargain was
made between them ; and as night drew on, each went
early to his bed.

III

NEXT morn, full early before the day, all the folk
of the castle up-rise, and saddle their horses,
and truss their saddle-bags. The noble lord of the
castle too arrays himself for riding, eats a sop hastily,
and goes to mass. Before daylight, he and his men
are on their horses ; then the hounds are called out
and coupled ; three short notes are blown by the
bugles, and a hundred hunters join in the chase. To
their stations the deer-stalkers go, and the hounds are
cast off, and joyously the chase begins.

Roused by the clamour the deer rush to the heights,
but are soon driven back ; the harts and bucks are
allowed to pass, but the hinds and does are driven back
to the shade. As they fly they are shot by the bowmen : the hounds and the hunters, with a loud cry,
follow in pursuit, and those that escape the arrows are
killed by the hounds. The lord waxes joyful in the
chase, which lasted till the approach of night.

All this time, Sir Gawayne lay abed,—and woke
only to hear afar the baying of the hounds, and so to

doze again. But at length there befell a knock at his door, and a damsel entered to bid him rise, and come to meat with her mistress. Straightway he arose, attired himself, put the fair ring on his finger, that his host had given him and descended to greet the lady of the castle.

"Good-morrow, fair sir," says she, "you are a late sleeper, I see!" She tells him, with a laughing glance, that she doubts if he really be Sir Gawayne that all the world worships: for he cares better to sleep than to hunt with the knights in the wood, or talk with the ladies in their bower.

"In good faith," quoth Sir Gawayne, "save this ring on my finger, there is nought I would not yield thee in token of my service and thy courtesy."

The lady told him that if true courtesy were enclosed in himself, he would keep back nothing,—no, not so much as a ring! But Sir Gawayne bethought him of his word to the lord of the castle; of his promise also to the Green Knight. He may not, he says, yield up his ring; but he will be forever her true servant.

We leave now the lady and Sir Gawayne, and turn to tell how the lord of the land and his men end their hunt in wood and heath. Of the killed a "quarry" they make; and set about "breaking" the deer, and take away the "assay" or fat; and rend off the hide. When all is ready, they feed the hounds, and then they make for home.

Anon Sir Gawayne hearing them approach the castle, goes out to meet his host. Then the lord commands all his household to assemble, and the venison to be brought before him ; he calls Gawayne, and asks him whether he does not deserve much praise for his success in the chase. When the knight has said that fairer venison he has not seen in winter,— nay, not this seven year,—his host doth bid him take the whole, according to the agreement between them made last night. Gawayne gives the knight a comely kiss in return, and his host desires to know if he too has gotten much weal at home ?

" Nay," says Sir Gawayne, " ask me no more of that ! "

Thereupon the lord of the castle laughed, and they went to supper, where were dainties new, enough and to spare. Anon they are sitting by the hearth, while wine is carried round, and again Sir Gawayne and his host renew their compact, as before, and so they take leave of each other and hasten to bed.

Scarce had the cock cackled thrice on the morrow, when the lord was up, and again with his hunters and horns out and abroad, pursuing the chase. The hunters cheer on the hounds, which fall to the scent, forty at once ; all come together by the side of a cliff, and look about on all sides, beating the bushes. Out there rushes a fierce wild boar, who fells three to the ground with the first thrust. Full quickly the hunters pursue him ; however, he attacks the hounds,

causing them to yowl and yell. The bowmen send
their arrows after this wild beast, but they glide off,
shivered in pieces. Enraged with the blows, he
attacks the hunters : then the lord of the land blows
his bugle, and pursues the boar.

All this time, Sir Gawayne lies abed, as on the
previous day, according to his promise. And again,
when he is summoned out of his late slumbers, the
lady of the castle twits him with his lack of courtesy.

" Sir," says she, " if ye indeed be Sir Gawayne, me-
thinkest you would not have forgotten that which
yesterday I taught ! "

" What is that ? " quoth he.

" That I taught you of giving," says she ; " yet,
you give not the ring as courtesy requires."

" Poor is the gift," he says, " that is not given
of free will ! "

But then the lady takes a ring from her own finger,
and bids him to keep it. " And I would hear from
you," she says, " some stories of beautiful dames, and
of feats of arms and the deeds that become true
knights."

Sir Gawayne says he has no sleight in the telling
of such tales, and he may not take the ring she would
give him, but he would for ever be her servant.

Meanwhile, the lord pursued the wild boar, that
bit the backs of his hounds asunder, and caused the
stoutest of his hunters to start back. At last the
beast was too exhausted to run any more and entered

a hole in a rock, by the side of a brook, the froth foaming at his mouth. None durst approach him, so many had he torn with his tusks. The knight, seeing the boar at bay, alights from his horse, and seeks to attack him with his sword ; the boar rushes out upon the man, who, aiming well, wounds him in the side, and the wild beast is killed by the hounds.

Then was there blowing of horns and baying of hounds. One, wise in wood-craft, begins to unlace the boar, and hews off the head. Then he feeds his hounds ; and the two halves of the carcase are next bound together and hung upon a pole. The boar's head is now borne before the lord of the castle, who hastens home.

Gawayne is called upon, when the hunt returns, to receive the spoil, and the lord of the land is well pleased when he sees him ; and shows him the wild boar, and tells him of its length and breadth. " Such a brawn of a beast," Sir Gawayne says he never has seen. To Gawayne then the wild boar is given, according to the covenant ; and in return he kisses his host, who declares his guest to be the best he knows.

Tables are raised aloft, cloths laid upon them, and waxen torches are lighted. With much mirth and glee, supper is served in the hall. When they had long played in the hall, they went to the upper chamber, where they drank and discoursed. Sir Gawayne at length begs leave of his host to depart on the morrow ;

but his host swears to him that he must stay, and come
to the Green Chapel on New Year's morn long before
prime. So Gawayne consents to remain for another
night; and full still and softly he sleeps throughout it.

Early in the morning the lord of the castle is up;
after mass, a morsel he takes with his men to break his
fast. Then were they all mounted on their horses
before the hall-gates, and ready for the hunt. It was
a clear, frosty morning when they rode off, and the
hunters, dispersed by a wood's side, came upon the
track of a fox, which was followed up by the hounds.
And now they get sight of the game, and pursue him
through many a rough grove. The fox at last leaps
over a spinney, and by a rugged path seeks to get
clear from the hounds; he comes upon one of the
hunting-stations, where he is attacked by the dogs.
However, he slips them, and makes again for the
woods. Then was it fine sport to listen to the hounds,
and the hallooing of the hunters; there the fox was
threatened, and called a thief. But Reynard was wily,
and led them far astray over brake and spinney.

Meanwhile, Sir Gawayne, left at home, soundly
sleeps within his comely curtains. At length the lady
of the castle, clothed in a rich mantle, comes to his
chamber, opens a window, and reproaches him :—

"Ah! man, how canst thou sleep; this morning
is so clear?"

Sir Gawayne was, when she aroused him, dreaming
of his forthcoming adventure at the Green Chapel, but

he started up, and greeted his fair visitor. Again, as
she had done before, she desired some gift by which to
remember him when he was gone.

"Now, sir," she entreats him, "now before thy
departing, do me this courtesy!"

Sir Gawayne tells her that she is worthy of a
far better gift than he can bestow. He has no men
laden with trunks containing precious things.

Thereupon again the lady of the castle offers him
a gold ring, but he refuses to accept it, as he has none
that he is free to give in return. Very sorrowful was
she on account of his refusal; she takes off her green
girdle, and beseeches him to take it. Gawayne again
refuses to accept anything, but promises, "ever in hot
and in cold, to be her true servant."

"Do you refuse it," says the lady, "because
it is simple? Whoso knew the virtues that it
possesses would highly prize it. For he who is
girded with this green girdle cannot be wounded or
slain."

Thereupon Sir Gawayne thinks of his adventure
at the Green Chapel, and when she again earnestly
presses him to take the girdle, he consents not only to
take it, but to keep the possession of it a secret. Then
she takes her leave; Gawayne hides the girdle, and
then hies to the chapel, and asks pardon for any
misdeeds he has ever done. When he returns to the
hall, he makes himself so merry among the ladies with
comely songs and carols, that they said : " This knight

was so merry never before, since hither he came to the castle ! "

Meanwhile the lord of the castle was still in the field ; he had already slain the fox. He had spied Reynard coming through a " rough grove " and tried to strike him with his sword ; but the fox was seized by one of the hounds. The rest of the hunters hastened thither, with horns full many, for it was the merriest meet that ever was heard ; and carrying the fox's skin and brush they all ride home. The lord at last alights at his dear home, where he finds Sir Gawayne amusing the ladies ; the knight comes forward and welcomes his host, and according to covenant kisses him thrice.

" My faith ! " says the other, " ye have had much bliss ! I have hunted all day and have gotten nothing but the skin of this foul fox, a poor reward for three such kisses." He then tells him how the fox was slain ; and with much mirth and minstrelsy they made merry until the time came for them to part. Gawayne takes leave of his host, and thanks him for his happy sojourn. He asks for a man to teach him the way to the Green Chapel. A servant is assigned him, and then he takes leave of the ladies, kissing them sorrowfully. They commend him to Christ. He then departs, thanking each one he meets for his service and solace ; he retires to rest, but sleeps little, for much has he to think of on the morrow. Let him lie there, and be still awhile, and I will tell what next befell him.

IV

Now New Year's Day has drawn nigh, and the
weather is stormy. Snow falls and the dale is full of
deep drift. Gawayne in his bed hears each cock that
crows ; he calls for the chamberlain, and bids him
bring his armour. Men knock off the rust from his
rich habergeon, and the knight then calls for his steed.
While he clothed himself in his rich garments, he
forgot not the girdle, the lady's gift, but with it
doubly girded his loins ; he wore it not for its rich
ornaments, " but to save himself when it behoved him
to suffer." All the people of the castle he thanked full
oft, and then was his steed Gringolet arrayed, full
ready to prick on. Sir Gawayne returns thanks for
the honour and kindness shown to him by all, and
then he steps into the saddle from the mounting-stone,
and says, " This castle to Christ I commend ; may He
give it ever good chance ! "

Therewith the castle gates are opened, and the
knight rides forth, and goes on his way accompanied
by his guide. They ride by rocky ways and cliffs,
where each hill wore a hat of cloud and a mist-cloak,
and when it is full daylight, they find themselves " on
a hill full high." Then his guide bade Sir Gawayne
abide, saying,—

" I have brought you hither, and ye are not now far
from the appointed place. Full perilous is it esteemed,

its lord is fierce and stern, his body is bigger than the
best four in King Arthur's house; none passes by the
Green Chapel that he does not ding to death with dint
of his hand, for be it churl or chaplain, monk, mass-
priest or any man else, he kills them all.   He has lived
there long, and against his sore dints ye may not
defend you; wherefore, good Sir Gawayne, let this
man alone, and go by some other region, and I swear
faithfully that I will never say that ever ye attempted
to flee from any man."

Gawayne replies that to shun this danger would
mark him as a coward knight; to the chapel, therefore, he will go, though the lord thereof were the
cruellest and strongest of men.

"Full well," says he, "can God devise how to save
His true servants!"

"Marry," quoth the other, "since it pleases thee to
lose thy life, take thy helmet on thy head, and thy
spear in thy hand, and ride down this path by yon
rock-side, till thou come to the bottom of the valley.
Look a little to the left, and thou shalt see the chapel
itself and the man that guards it."

Having thus spoken, the guide takes leave of the
knight.   "By God's grace," says Sir Gawayne, "I
will neither weep nor groan.   To God's will I am full
ready to bow!"   So on he rides, through the dale,
and eagerly looks about him.   He sees, however, no
sign of a resting-place, but only high and steep banks,
no chapel can he discern anywhere.   At last he sees a

Here we are alone ; have off thy helmet and take thy pay at once.

hill by the side of a stream ; thither he goes, alights, and fastens his horse to the branch of a tree. He walks round the hill, looking for the chapel, and debating with himself what it might be, and at last he comes upon an old cave in the crag. "Truly," he reflects, "a wild place is here—a fitting place for the Green Knight to make his devotions in evil fashion ; if this be the chapel it is the most cursed kirk that ever I saw."

But with that, he hears a loud noise, from beyond the brook. It clattered like the grinding of a scythe on a grindstone, and whirred like a mill-stream.

"'Though my life I forego," says Gawayne, "no noise shall terrify me." And he cried aloud, "Who dwells here and will hold discourse with me." Then he heard a loud voice commanding him to abide where he stood, and soon there came out of a hole, with a fell weapon—a Danish axe, quite new—the Green Knight clothed just as Gawayne saw him long before. When he reached the stream, he leapt over it, and striding on, he met Sir Gawayne without the least obeisance.

" God preserve thee ! " he says, "as a true knight thou hast timed thy travel. Thou knowest the covenant between us, that on New Year's Day I should return thy blow. Here we are alone ; have off thy helmet and take thy pay at once."

" By my faith," quoth Sir Gawayne, " I shall not begrudge thee thy will."

Then he shows his bare neck, and appears undaunted.

The Green Knight seizes his grim weapon, and with all his force raises it aloft. As it came gliding down, Sir Gawayne shrank a little with his shoulders, then the other reproved him, saying, "Thou art not that Gawayne that is so good esteemed, for thou fleest for fear before thou feelest harm. I never flinched when thou struckest; my head flew to my foot, yet I never fled; wherefore I ought to be called the better man."

"I flinched once," says Gawayne, "but will no more. Bring me to the point; deal me my death-blow at once."

"Have at thee, then," says the other, and with that, prepares to aim the fatal blow. Gawayne never flinches, but stands as still as a stone.

"Now," says the Green Knight, "I must strike thee, since thy heart is whole."

"Strike on," says the other. Then the Green Knight makes ready to strike, and lets fall his axe on the bare neck of Sir Gawayne. The sharp weapon pierced the flesh so that the blood flowed. When Gawayne saw the blood on the snow, he unsheathed his sword, and thus he spake,—

"Cease, man, of thy blow. If thou givest me any more, blow for blow shall I requite thee! We agreed only upon one stroke."

The Green Knight rested on his axe, looked at Sir Gawayne, who appeared bold and fearless, and addressed him as follows,—

"Bold knight, be not so wroth, I promised thee a

stroke, and thou hast it. Be satisfied ; I could have dealt worse with thee ; I menaced thee first with one blow for the covenant between us on the first night. Another I aimed at thee because of the second night. A true man should restore truly, and then he need fear no harm. Thou failed at the third time, and therefore take thee that stroke, for my girdle (woven by my wife) thou wearest. I know thy secret, and my wife's gift to thee, for I sent her to try thee, and faultless I found thee : but yet thou sinnedst a little, since thou tookest the girdle to save thy skin and for love of thy life."

Sir Gawayne stands there confounded before the Green Knight.

"Cursed," he says, "be cowardice and covetousness both ! "

Then he takes off the girdle, and throws it to the Green Knight, and confesses himself to have been guilty of untruth. Then the other, laughing, thus spoke,—

"Thou art confessed so clean, that I hold thee as free, as if thou hadst never been guilty. I give thee, Sir Gawayne, the gold-hemmed girdle as a token of thy adventure at the Green Chapel. Come again to my castle, and abide there for the remainder of the New Year's festival."

"Nay, forsooth," says Gawayne, "I have sojourned sadly, but bliss betide thee! Commend me to your comely wife, who beguiled me ; but though I be now beguiled, methinks I should be excused! God reward you for your girdle! I will wear it in remembrance of my fault, and when pride shall prick me, one look upon this green band shall abate it. But tell me your right name, and I shall have done."

The Green Knight replies, " I am called Bernlak de Hautdesert, through the might of Morgan le Fay, the pupil of Merlin ; she can tame even the haughtiest. It was she who caused me to test the renown of the Round Table, hoping to grieve Queen Guenever, and cause her death through fear. Morgan le Fay is even thine aunt ; therefore come to her, and make merry in my house."

But Sir Gawayne refused to return with the Green Knight. He bade him a courteous farewell, and then he turned Gringolet's head again toward Arthur's hall. By wild ways and lonely places did he ride. Sometimes he harboured in a house by night, and sometimes he had to shift under the trees. The wound in his neck became whole, but he still carried about him the belt in token of his fault.

Thus Sir Gawayne comes again at last to the Court of King Arthur, and great was the joy of them all to see him. The king and his knights ask him concerning his journey, and Gawayne tells them of his adventures, and of the Green Knight's castle and the lady, and lastly, of the girdle that he wore. He showed them the cut in his neck, and as he groaned for grief and shame, the blood rushed to his face.

"Lo!" says he, handling the green girdle, "this is the band of blame, a token of my cowardice and covetousness. I must needs wear it as long as I live."

The king comforts the knight, and all the Court too. Each knight of the brotherhood agrees to wear a bright green belt for Gawayne's sake, who evermore honoured it. Thus in Arthur's day this adventure befell. May He who bore the crown of thorns, bring us to His bliss! Amen.

H.C '06

THE GREEN CHILDREN

THAT was a wonderful thing that happened at St. Mary's of the Wolf-pits. A boy and his sister were found by the country folk of that place near the mouth of a pit, who had limbs like those of men ; but the colour of their skin wholly differed from that of you and me and the people of our upper world, for it was tinged all of a green colour.

No one could understand the speech of the Green Children. When they were brought to the house of a certain knight, Sir Richard de Calne, they wept bitterly. Bread and honey and milk were set before them, but they would not touch any of these, though they were tormented by great hunger. At length, some beans fresh-cut were brought, stalks and all, into the house, and the children made signs, with great avidity, that the green food should be given to them. Thereupon they seized on it, and opened the bean-stalks instead of the pods, thinking the beans were in the hollow of the stem ; and not finding anything of the kind there, they began to weep anew. When the pods were opened and the naked beans offered to them, they fed on these with great delight, and for a long time they would taste no other food.

The people of their country, they said, and all that was to be seen in that country, were of a green colour. Neither did any sun shine there ; but instead of it they enjoyed a softer light like that which shines after sunset. Being asked how they came into our upper world, they said that as they were following their green flocks, they came to a great cavern ; and on entering it they heard a delightful sound of bells. Ravished by its sweetness, they went for a long time wandering on and on through the cavern until they came to its mouth. When they came out of it, they were struck senseless by the glaring light of the sun, and the summer warmth of the air ; and they thus lay for a long time ; then, being awaked, they were terrified by the noise of those who had come upon them; they wished to fly, but they could not find again the entrance of the cavern, and so were they caught.

.   .   .   .

If you ask what became of the Green Children, I cannot tell you, for no one seems to know right clearly. Perchance they found their cave, and went back again to the Green Country, as the mermaid goes back at last to the sea.

The Story of the Fairy Horn

NCE upon a time there was a knight that had a Wyvern[1] on his shield ; but he was none the better for that, as you shall hear.

One day as he was riding in the country beyond Gloucester, he came to a forest abounding in boars, stags, and every kind of wild beast. Now in a grovy lawn of this forest there was a little mount, rising in a point to the height of a man, on which knights and other hunters were used to ascend when

[1] A Wyvern was a kind of dragon with two legs and a curled, or rather coiled, tail.

fatigued with heat and thirst, to seek some relief. The nature of the place—for it is a fairy place—is, however, such that whoever ascends the mount must leave his companions, and go quite alone.

As the knight rode in the wood, and came nigh this fairy-knoll, he met with a wood-cutter and questioned him about it. He must go thither alone, the wood-cutter told him, and say, as if speaking to some other person,—

"I thirst!"

Immediately there would appear a cup-bearer in a rich crimson dress, with a shining face, bearing in his stretched-out hand a large horn, adorned with gold and gems, such as was the custom among the most ancient English. The cup was full of nectar, of an unknown but most delicious flavour, and when it was drunk, all heat and weariness fled from those who drank of it, so that they became ready to toil anew, instead of being tired from having toiled. Moreover, when the nectar was drunk, the cup-bearer offered a towel to the drinker, to wipe his mouth with, and then having done this courtesy, he waited neither for a silver penny for his services, nor for any question to be asked.

Now the knight with the Wyvern laughed to himself when he heard this.

"Who," thought he, "would be fool enough, having within his grasp such a drinking-horn, ever to let it go again from him!"

Later, that very same day, as he rode back hot and tired and thirsty from his hunting, he bethought him

of the fairy-knoll and the fairy-horn. Sending away
his followers, he repaired thither all alone, and did as
the wood-cutter had told him. He ascended the little
hill, and said in a bold voice,—

"I thirst!"

Instantly there appeared, as the wood-cutter had
foretold, a cup-bearer in a crimson dress, bearing in his
hand a drinking-horn. The horn was richly beset with
precious gems ; and the knight was filled with envy at
sight of it. No sooner had he seized upon it, and tasted
of its delicious nectar, which glowed in his veins, than
he determined when he had drained it to make off with
the horn. So, having gotten the horn, and drunk of it
every drop, instead of returning it to the cup-bearer, as
in good manners he should have done, he stepped down
from the knoll, and rudely made off with it in his hand.

But, learn ye then what fate overtook this knight
that bore the Wyvern on his shield, but was without
true knighthood, and robbed the Fairy Horn. For
the good Earl of Gloucester, who had often quenched
his thirst, and restored his strength, standing on the
fairy-knoll, when he heard that the wicked knight had
destroyed the kind custom of the horn, attacked the
robber in his stronghold, and forthright slew him, and
carried off the horn. But alas ! the earl did not return
it to the fairy-cupbearer, but gave it to his master and
lord, King Henry the Elder. Since then you may
stand all day at the fairy-knoll, and many times cry " I
thirst !" but you may not taste of the Fairy Horn.

THE LADY MOLE

A LONELY life for the dark and silent mole! Day is to her night. She glides along her narrow vaults, unconscious of the glad and glorious scenes of earth and air and sea. She was born, as it were, in a grave; and in one long, living sepulchre she dwells and dies. Is not existence to her a kind of doom? Wherefore is she thus a dark, sad exile from the blessed light of day? Hearken!

Here, in our bleak old Cornwall, the first mole was once a lady of the land. Her abode was in the far west, among the hills of Morwenna, beside the Severn Sea. She was the daughter of a lordly race, the only child of her mother, and the father of the house was dead: her name was Alice of the Combe. Fair was she and comely, tender and tall; and she stood upon the threshold of her youth. But most of all did men marvel at the glory of her large blue eyes. They were, to look upon, like the summer waters, when the sea is soft with light. They were to her mother a joy, and to the maiden herself, ah, benedicite! a pride. She trusted in the loveliness of those eyes, and in her face and features and form; and so it was that the damsel was wont to pass the whole summer day in the choice of rich apparel and precious stones and gold. Howbeit this was one of the ancient and common usages of those old departed days. Now, in the fashion of her stateliness and in the hue and texture of her garments, there was none among the maidens of old Cornwall like Alice of the Combe. Men sought her far and near, but she was to them all, like a form of graven stone, careless and cold. Her soul was set upon a Granville's love, fair Sir Beville of Stowe—the flower of the Cornish chivalry—that noble gentleman! That valorous knight! he was her star. And well might she wait upon his eyes; for he was the garland of the west. The loyal soldier of a Stuart king—he was that stately Granville who lived a hero's life and died a

Stood before the mirrored glass.

warrior's death! He was her star. Now there was a
signal made of banquet in the halls of Stowe, of wassail
and dance. The messenger had sped, and Alice of the
Combe would be there. Robes, precious and many,
were unfolded from their rest, and the casket poured
forth jewel and gem, that the maiden might stand
before the knight victorious. It was the day—the
hour—the time—her mother sat at her wheel by the
hearth—the page waited in the hall—she came down in
her loveliness, into the old oak room, and stood before
the mirrored glass—her robe was of woven velvet, rich
and glossy and soft; jewels shone like stars in the
midnight of her raven hair, and on her hand there
gleamed afar off a bright and glorious ring! She stood
—she gazed upon her own fair countenance and form,
and worshipped! "Now all good angels succour thee,
my Alice, and bend Sir Beville's soul! Fain am I to
greet thee wedded wife before I die! I do yearn to
hold thy children on my knee! Often shall I pray
to-night that the Granville heart may yield! Ay, thy
victory shall be thy mother's prayer." "Prayer!" was
the haughty answer, "now, with the eyes that I see
in that glass, and with this vesture meet for a queen, I
lack no trusting prayer!" Saint Juliet shield us!
Ah! words of fatal sound—there was a sudden shriek,
a sob, a cry, and where was Alice of the Combe?
Vanished, silent, gone! They had heard wild tones of
mystic music in the air, there was a rush, a beam of
light, and she was gone, and that for ever! East

sought they her, and west, in northern parts and south;
but she was never more seen in the land. Her
mother wept till she had not a tear left; none sought
to comfort her, for it was vain. Moons waxed and
waned, and the crones by the cottage hearth had whiled
away many a shadowy night with tales of Alice of the
Combe. But at the last, as the gardener in the pleasaunce leaned one day on his spade, he saw among the
roses a small round hillock of earth, such as he had
never seen before, and upon it something which shone.
It was her ring! It was the very jewel she had worn
the day she vanished out of sight! They looked
earnestly upon it, and they saw within the border, for
it was wide, the tracery of certain small fine runes, in
the ancient Cornish tongue, which said,—

> " Beryan erde
> Ayn und perde ! "

Then came the priest of the place of Morwenna, a
grey and silent man. He had served long years at his
lonely altar, a worn and solitary form. But he had
been wise in language in his youth, and men said that
he heard and understood voices in the air when spirits
speak and glide. He read and he interpreted thus the
legend on the ring,—

> " The earth must hide
> Both eyes and pride ! "

Now as on a day he uttered these words, in the
pleasaunce, by the mound, on a sudden there was

among the grass a low faint cry. They beheld, and oh, wondrous and strange! There was a small dark creature, clothed in a soft velvet skin in texture and in hue like the Lady Alice her robe, and they saw, as it groped into the earth, that it moved along without eyes, in everlasting night! Then the ancient man wept, for he called to mind many things and saw what they meant ; and he showed them how that this was the maiden, who had been visited with a doom for her pride! Therefore her rich array had been changed into the skin of a creeping thing, and her large proud eyes were sealed up, and she herself had become—

THE FIRST MOLE OF THE HILLOCKS OF CORNWALL!

Ah, woe is me and well-a-day! that damsel so stately and fair, sweet Lady Alice of the Combe, should become, for a judgment, the dark mother of the moles! Now take ye good heed, Cornish maidens, how ye put on vain apparel to win love! And cast down your eyes, all ye damsels of the west, and look meekly on the ground! Be ye ever good and gentle, tender and true ; and when ye see your own image in the glass, and ye begin to be lifted up with the loveliness of that shadowy thing, call to mind the maiden of the vale of Morwenna, her noble eyes and comely countenance, her vesture of price, and the glittering ring! Sit ye by the wheel as of old they sate, and when ye draw forth the lengthening wool, sing ye evermore and say,—

> " Beryan erde
> Ayn und perde !"

CATSKIN

I

NCE upon a time there was a little girl who, when she came into the world, found she was not wanted there, for her father had long wished for a son and heir, and when a daughter was born instead, he fell into a blind rage and said, "She sha'n't stay long in my house!"

Her mother became very sad at this, and fearing her father's hatred, sent away the poor little babe to a foster-nurse, who lived in a house by a great oak wood. There the child lived till she was fifteen summers old. Then her old foster-mother died, but before she died, she told the poor child at her bedside, to hide all her pretty white frocks in the wood by the crystal waterfall that sounded there all day long among the oak leaves. Then she was to put on a dress of catskin the old dame gave her, and go and seek a place as a servant-maid far away in the town.

Catskin (for so she must now be called) did as the

old dame had told her, and presently set off all alone in her travels. She wandered a long way, and at last came to the town, and to a great house. There she knocked at the gate, and begged the porter for a place as a servant. He sent her upstairs then to speak to the lady of the house, who looked hard at poor Catskin, and patted her on the head, and ended by saying,—

"I'm sorry I've no better place for you, my dear, but you can be a scullion under the cook, if you like!"

So Catskin was put under the cook, and a very sad life she led with her, for as often as the cook got out of temper she took a ladle and broke it over poor Catskin's head. Well, time went on and there was to be a grand ball in the town.

"Oh, Mrs. Cook," said Catskin, "how much I should like to go!"

"You go, with your catskin robe, among the fine ladies and lords, you dirty slut, a very fine figure you'd make!" And with that she took a basin of water and dashed it in poor Catskin's face.

But Catskin briskly shook her ears and went off to her hiding-place in the wood; and there, as the old song says,—

> "She washed every stain from her skin,
>   In some crystal waterfall;
> Then put on a beautiful dress,
>   And hasted away to the ball."

II

WHEN she entered the ladies were mute, overcome by her beauty; but the lord, her young master, at once fell in love with her. He prayed her to be his partner in the dance. To this Catskin said "Yes," with a sweet smile. All that evening with no other partner but Catskin would he dance.

"Pray tell me, fair maid," he said at last, "where you live?" For now was the sad parting time; but no other answer would she give him than this distich,—

> *"Kind sir, if the truth I must tell,*
> *At the sign of the Basin of Water I dwell."*

Then Catskin flew from the ballroom and put on her furry robe again, and slipt into the kitchen unseen by the cook, who little thought where her scullion had been. The very next day the young squire told his mother he would never rest till he'd found out this beautiful maid, and who she was, and where she lived.

Well, time went on, and another grand ball was to be given in the town. When Catskin heard of it,— "Mrs. Cook, oh, Mrs. Cook," she cried, "how much I should like to go!"

"You go with your catskin robe among the fine lords and ladies, you dirty slut! a very fine figure you'd make!" And in a great rage she took the ladle and struck poor Catskin's head a terrible blow.

But off went Catskin, none the worse, shaking her ears, and swift to her forest she fled. And there as the old song says,—

> "She washed every blood-stain off,
> In some crystal waterfall ;
> Put on a more beautiful dress,
> And hasted away to the ball."

III

Now at the ballroom door the young squire was in waiting ; he longed to see nothing so much as the beautiful Catskin again. When she arrived he asked her to dance, and again she said "Yes" with the same smiling look as before.

And again all the night he would have none but pretty Catskin for his partner.

"Pray tell me," said he, presently, "where you live ? " for now the time came for parting.

But Catskin no other answer would give than this distich,—

> "*Kind sir, if the truth I must tell,*
> *At the sign of the Broken-Ladle I dwell.*"

Then she flew from the ball, put on her catskin robe under the dark oak trees, and slipt back into the kitchen unseen by the cook, who little thought where she had been.

But now the grandest ball of the whole year was to be held in the town. And just as she had done before, when Catskin heard of it, she resolved that go she must, Mrs. Cook or no Mrs. Cook.

"Mrs. Cook," said Catskin to her one evening, "have you heard of the grand ball? How much I should like to go!"

"You go?" said Mistress Cook as before, "with your catskin robe, you impudent girl! among the fine ladies and lords, a very fine figure you'd cut."

In a fury she snatched up the skimmer, and broke it on Catskin's head; but heart-whole and as lively as ever, away to the oakwood Catskin flew; and there, as the old song says,—

> "She washed the stains of blood,
>   In the crystal waterfall;
>   Then put on her most beautiful dress,
>   And hastened away to the ball."

IV

At the ball-room door the young squire stood waiting, dressed in a velvet coat. He longed to see nothing so much as the beautiful Catskin again. When he asked her to dance, she agreed with a smile, and again all the night long, with none but fair Catskin would he dance.

"Pray tell me, fair maid, where you live?" he asked her when the parting-time came; but she had no other answer for him than this distich,—

> "*Kind sir, if the truth I must tell,*
>   *At the sign of the Broken-Skimmer I dwell.*"

V

THEN she flew from the ball to the oakwood, and threw on her catskin cloak again. She slipt into the house unseen by the cook, but not unseen by the young squire; for this time he had followed too fast, and hid himself in the forest, and saw the strange disguise she put on there.

Next day he took to his bed and sent for the doctor to come, and said he should die if Catskin did not come to see him. Well, Catskin was sent for, and he told her how dearly he loved her; indeed, if she did not love him, his heart would break.

Then the doctor, who knew how proud the old lady his mother was, promised to ask her consent to their wedding. Had she not feared her son would die, her pride would never have yielded; but after a hard struggle she said " Yes! "

The sick young squire got quickly well, when he heard this good tidings. And so it was Catskin, before a twelvemonth was gone, when the oakwood grew green again, was married to him, and they lived happily for ever after.

Be bold, be bold, but not too bold,
Lest that your heart's blood should run cold.

M^R,, FOX

"Like the old tale, my Lord : it is not so, nor 'twas not so ; but indeed, God forbid it should be so."
Much Ado About Nothing.

ONCE upon a time there was a young lady called Lady Mary, who had two brothers. One summer they all three went to a country seat of theirs, which they had not before visited. Among the other gentry in the neighbourhood who came to see them was a Mr. Fox, a bachelor, with whom they, and the young lady particularly, were much pleased. He used

86

often to dine with them, and frequently invited Lady
Mary to come and see his house. One day that her
brothers were absent elsewhere, and she had nothing
better to do, she determined to go thither, and
accordingly set out unattended. When she arrived at
the house and knocked at the door, no one answered.

At length she opened it and went in ; over the
portal of the door was written,—

    " Be bold, be bold, but not too bold."

She went on ; over the staircase was the same
inscription,—

    " Be bold, be bold, but not too bold."

She went up ; over the entrance of a gallery was
the same again,—

    " Be bold, be bold, but not too bold."

Still she went on, and over the door of a chamber
found written,—

    " Be bold, be bold, but not too bold,
    Lest that your heart's blood should run cold ! "

Lady Mary opened it ; it was full of skeletons.
She retreated in haste, and, coming downstairs, saw
from a window Mr. Fox advancing towards the house
with a drawn sword in one hand, while with the other

he dragged along a young lady by her hair. She had just time to slip down and hide herself under the stairs before Mr. Fox and his victim arrived at the foot of them. As he pulled the young lady upstairs, she caught hold of one of the banisters with her hand, on which was a rich bracelet. Mr. Fox cut it off with his sword. The hand and bracelet fell into Lady Mary's lap, who then contrived to escape unobserved, and got safe home to her brothers' house.

A few days afterwards Mr. Fox came to dine with them as usual. After dinner the guests began to amuse each other with stories and strange anecdotes, and Lady Mary said she would relate to them a remarkable dream she had lately had.

" I dreamt," said she, " that as you, Mr. Fox, had often invited me to your house, I would go there one morning. When I came to the house I knocked at the door, but no one answered. When I opened the door, over the hall I saw written,—

" ' Be bold, be bold, but not too bold.'

But," said she, turning to Mr. Fox, and smiling, " it is not so, nor it was not so."

She pursued the rest of the story in the same way, concluding at every turn with " it is not so, nor it was not so," till she came to the room full of skeletons, when Mr. Fox took up the burden of the tale, and said,—

Whereupon the guests drew their swords.

> "It is not so, nor it was not so,
> And God forbid it should be so!"—

He continued to repeat this at every further turn of the dreadful tale, till she came to the cutting-off the young lady's hand, when, upon his saying, as usual,—

> "It is not so, nor it was not so,
> And God forbid it should be so!"—

Lady Mary retorts by saying,—

> "But it is so, and it was so,
> And here the hand I have to show!"—

at the same moment producing the hand and bracelet from her lap, whereupon the guests drew their swords and instantly cut Mr. Fox into a thousand pieces.

"TOM TIT TOT"

NCE upon a time there were a woman, and she baked five pies. And when they come out of the oven, they was that overbaked the crust were too hard to eat. So she says to her darter,—

"Maw'r,"[1] says she, "put you them there pies on the shelf, an' leave 'em there a little, an' they'll come again."—She meant, you know, the crust would get soft.

But the gal, she says to herself : " Well, if they'll come agin, I'll ate 'em now." And she set to work and ate 'em all, first and last.

Well, come supper-time, the woman she said : "Goo you, and git one o' them there pies. I dare say they've come agin now."

The gal she went an' she looked, and there warn't nothin' but the dishes. So back she come and says she : "Noo, they ain't come agin."

"Not none on 'em?" says the mother.

[1] Lass, girl.

" Not none on 'em," says she.

" Well, come agin, or not come agin," says the woman, " I'll ha' one for supper."

" But you can't, if they ain't come," says the gal.

" But I can," says she.   " Goo you and bring the best of 'em."

" Best or worst," says the gal, " I've ate 'em all, and you can't ha' one till that's come agin."

Well, the woman she were wholly bate,[1] and she took her spinnin' to the door to spin, and as she span she sang,—

> " My darter ha' ate five, five pies to-day.
> My darter ha' ate five, five pies to-day."

The king he were a-comin' down the street, an' he heard her sing, but what she sang he couldn't hear, so he stopped and said,—

" What were that you was a-singing of, maw'r ? "

The woman she were ashamed to let him hear what her darter had been a-doing', so she sang, 'stids[2] o' that,—

> " My darter ha' spun five, five skeins to-day.
> My darter ha' spun five, five skeins to-day."

" S'ars o' mine ! " said the king, " I never heerd tell of any one as could do that."

Then he said : " Look you here, I want a wife, and I'll marry your darter.   But look you here," says

---

[1] Beaten.   [2] Instead.

he, " 'leven months out o' the year she shall have all the
vittles she likes to eat, and all the gowns she likes
to get, and all the company she likes to have ; but the
last month o' the year she'll ha' to spin five skeins
every day, an' if she doon't, I shall kill her."

"All right," says the woman ; for she thought
what a grand marriage that was. And as for them five
skeins, when it came to the time, there'd be plenty o'
ways of getting out of it, and likeliest, he'd ha' forgot
about it.

Well, so they was married. An' for 'leven months
the gal had all the vittles she liked to ate, and all the
gowns she liked to get, and all the company she
liked to have.

But when the time was gettin' oover, she began to
think about them there skeins an' to wonder if he had
'em in mind. But not one word did he say about 'em,
an' she wholly thought he'd forgot 'em.

But the last day o' the last month he takes her to
a room she'd never sets eyes on afore. There worn't
nothing in it but a spinnin'-wheel and a stool. An'
says he : "Now, my dear, here yow'll be shut in
to-morrow with some vittles and some flax, and if you
hain't spun five skeins by the night, your head will
goo off."

An' awa' he went about his business.

Well, she were that frightened, she'd allus been
such a useless mawther, that she didn't so much as
know how to spin, an' what were she to do to-morrow,

"The funniest little black thing you ever set eyes on."

with no one to come nigh her to help her. She sat down on a stool in the kitchen, and lawk! how she did cry!

However, all on a sudden she heard a sort of a knockin' low down on the door. She upped and oped it, an' what should she see but a small little black thing with a long tail. That looked up at her right curious, an' that said,—

"What are you a-cryin' for?"

"Wha's that to you?" says she.

"Never you mind," that said, "but tell me what you're a-cryin' for."

"That won't do me no good if I do," says she.

"You don't know that," that said, an' twirled that's tail round.

"Well," says she, "that won't do no harm, if that don't do no good," and she upped and told about the pies and the skeins, and everything.

"This is what I'll do," says the little black thing, "I'll come to your window every morning and take the flax and bring it spun at night."

"What's your pay?" says she.

That looked out o' the corner o' that's eyes, and that said: "I'll give you three guesses every night to guess my name, an' if you hain't guessed it afore the month's up, you shall be mine."

Well, she thought she'd be sure to guess that's name afore the month was up. "All right," says she, "I agree."

"All right," that says, an' lawk! how that twirled that's tail.

Well, the next day, the king he took her into the room, an' there was the flax an' the day's vittles.

"Now there's the flax," says he, "an' if that ain't spun up this night, off goes your head." An' then he went out an' locked the door.

He'd hardly gone when there was a knockin' on the window.

She upped and she oped it, and there sure enough was the little old thing a-settin' on the ledge.

"Where's the flax?" says he.

"Here it be," says she. And she gonned¹ it to him.

Well, in the evening a knockin' came again to the window. She upped and she oped it, and there were the little old thing with five skeins of flax on his arm.

"Here te be," says he, and he gonned it to her.

"Now, what's my name?" says he.

"What, is that Bill?" says she.

"Noo, that ain't," says he, an' he twirled his tail.

"Is that Ned?" says she.

"Noo, that ain't," says he, an' he twirled his tail.

"Well, is that Mark?" says she.

"Noo, that ain't," says he, an' he twirled his tail harder an' away he flew.

¹ Gave.

Well, when her husband he come in, there was the five skeins ready for him. " I see I sha'n't have for to kill you to-night, my dear," says he ; " you'll have your vittles and your flax in the mornin'," says he, an' away he goes.

Well, every day the flax an' the vittles they was brought, an' every day that there little black impet used for to come mornings and evenings. An' all the day the mawther she set a-trying for to think of names to say to it when it come at night. But she never hit on the right one. An' as it got towards the end o' the month, the impet that began for to look so maliceful, an' that twirled that's tail faster an' faster each time she gave a guess.

At last it came to the last day but one. The impet, that came at night along o' the five skeins, and that said,—

" What, ain't you got my name yet ? "

" Is that Nicodemus ? " says she.

" Noo, t'ain't," that says.

" Is that Sammle ? " says she.

" Noo, t'ain't," that says.

" A-well, is that Methusalem ? " says she.

" Noo, t'ain't that neither," that says.

Then that looks at her with that's eyes like a coal o' fire, an' that says : " Woman, there's only to morrow night, an' then you'll be mine ! " An' away it flew.

Well, she felt that horrid. Howsomeover, she

heard the king a-comin' along the passage. In he
came, an' when he see the five skeins, he says, says
he,—

"Well, my dear," says he, "I don't see but what
you'll have your skeins ready to-morrow night as well,
an' as I reckon I sha'n't have to kill you, I'll have
supper in here to-night." So they brought supper an'
another stool for him, and down the two they sat.

Well, he hadn't eat but a mouthful or so, when he
stops an' begins to laugh.

"What is it?" says she.

"A-why," says he, "I was out a huntin' to-day,
an' I got away to a place in the wood I'd never seen
afore. An' there was an old chalk-pit. An' I heard
a sort of a hummin', kind o'. So I got off my
hobby,[1] an' I went right quiet to the pit, an' I looked
down. Well, what should there be but the funniest
little black thing you ever set eyes on. An' what was
that a-doing on, but that had a little spinnin'-wheel, an'
that were a-spinnin' wonderful fast, an' a-twirlin' that's
tail. An' as that span, that sang :

> "'Nimmy Nimmy Not
> My name's TOM TIT TOT.'"

Well, when the mawther heard this, she fared as if
she could ha' jumped out of her skin for joy, but she
didn't say a word.

Next day that there little thing looked so maliceful

[1] Horse.

when he came for the flax. And when night came, she heard that a-knockin' on the window panes. She oped the window, an' that come right in on the ledge. That were grinnin' from ear to ear an' Oo! that's tail were twirlin' round so fast.

"What's my name?" that says, as that gonned her the skeins.

"Is that Solomon?" she says, pretendin' to be afeard.

"Noo, t'ain't," that says, and that come further into the room.

"Well, is that Zebedee?" says she again.

"Noo, t'ain't," says the impet. An' then that laughed an' twirled that's tail till you couldn't hardly see it.

"Take time, woman," that says; "next guess, and you're mine." An' that stretched out that's black hands at her.

Well, she backed a step or two, an' she looked at it, and then she laughed out, and says she, a-pointin' of her finger at it,—

"Nimmy Nimmy Not,
Yar name's TOM TIT TOT."

Well, when that heard her, that shrieked awful and away that flew into the dark, and she never saw it no more.

THE FAIRY BEGGAR

PLEASE, your grace, from out your store
   Give an alms to one that's poor,
That your mickle may have more.
Black I'm grown for want of meat;
Give me then an ant to eat,
Or the cleft ear of a mouse
Over-soured in drink of souce;

Or, sweet lady, reach to me
The abdomen of a bee ;
Flour of fuz-balls, that's too good
For a man in needy-hood :
But the meal of mill-dust can
Well content a craving man ;
Any arts the elves refuse
Well will serve the beggar's use.
But if this may seem too much
For an alms, then give me such
Little bits that nestle there
In the pris'ner's pannier.
So a blessing light upon
You and mighty Oberon :
That your plenty last till when
I return your alms again.

THE CAULD LAD OF HILTON

AT Hilton Hall, in the pleasant vale of the Wear, there used to be in the old days, a Brownie called The Cauld Lad. Every night the menservants who slept in the great hall heard him at work in the kitchen, knocking the things about if they had been set in order, or putting them straight, if the place was untidy. The servant-folk soon resolved to banish him if they could, and The Cauld Lad, who seemed to know of their design, was often heard singing in a melancholy tone,—

> " Wae's me ! wae's me !
> The acorn is not yet
> Fallen from the tree,
> That's to grow the wood,
> That's to make the cradle,
> That's to rock the bairn,
> That's to grow to a man,
> That's to lay me."

The maidservants, however, knew the old way of banishing a Brownie ; one night they left a green cloak and hood for The Cauld Lad by the kitchen fire, and remained on the watch. At midnight they saw him come in, gaze at the new clothes, try them on, and, apparently in great delight, go jumping and frisking about the kitchen.   But at the first crow of the cock he vanished crying,—

> " Here's a cloak, and here's a hood !
> The Cauld Lad of Hilton will do no more good ; "

and he never again returned to the kitchen ; yet it was said that he might still be heard at midnight singing those lines in a tone of melancholy.

There was one room at Hilton Hall long called the Cauld Lad's Room, and it was never occupied unless the house was full of company ; and many folk heard, late and early, The Cauld Lad wailing in the night :—

> " Here's a cloak, and here's a hood !
> The Cauld Lad of Hilton will do no more good ! "

H · C

" AINSEL "

ISTRESS ARMSTRONG, a canny widow, and her son Parcie,[1] who was a little boy then, lived together in a cottage near Rothley. One winter's night, Parcie refused to go to bed with his mother, as he wished to sit up for a while longer, "for," says he, "I am not a bit sleepy."

His mother told him that if he sat up by himself the old fairy-wife would most certainly come and take him away. But the boy laughed at this, and his mother went to bed, leaving him sitting by the fire.

He had not been there long, watching the fire and enjoying its ruddy blaze, when a bonny little figure, about the size of a bairn's doll, hopped down the chimney and alighted on the hearth. Parcie, poor little fellow, was like to be startled at first, but the Brownie's smile as it hopped to and fro before him soon overcame his fears. At last he inquired,—

"What do they ca' thou ?"

"Ainsel," answered the little thing, tossing its wee head.

[1] Percy.

HERBERT COLE. 1906.

So they began playing together like any two wee bairns ~

After a bit it turned to Parcie with just the same question :—"And what do they call thou?"

"*My* ainsel," answers Parcie.

So they began playing together like any two wee bairns. Their gambols went on till the fire began to grow dim ; when Parcie took up the poker to stir it, and a hot cinder accidentally fell upon the foot of his playmate. Her mouse voice was instantly raised to a most terrific yell, and Parcie had scarce time to crouch into the box-bed behind his mother, before the voice of the old fairy-wife was heard shouting,—

"Who's done it? Who's done it?"

"Hoots! it was 'my ainsel'!" said the boggart bairn.

"Why, then," said the mother, as she kicked her up the chimney, "what's all this noise for ; there's nyon (*i.e.*, no one) to blame but thine ainsel!"

THE FAIRY'S DINNER

A LITTLE mushroom-table spread,
　　After short prayers they set on bread,
A moon-parched grain of purest wheat
With some small glitt'ring grit, to eat
His choice bits with ; then in a trice
They make a feast less great than nice.
But all this while his eye is served,
We must not think his ear was starved ;
But that there was in place to stir
His spleen, the chirring grasshopper,
The merry cricket, puling fly,
The piping gnat for minstrelsy.
And now, we must imagine first,
The elves present, to quench his thirst,
A pure seed-pearl of infant dew,
Brought and besweetened in a blue
And fragrant violet ; which done,
His kitling eyes begin to run
Quite through the table, where he spies
The horns of papery butterflies,
Of which he eats ; and tastes a little
Of that we call the cuckoo's spittle.
A little fuz-ball pudding stands

By, yet not blessed by his hands,
That was too coarse ; but then forthwith
He ventures boldly on the pith
Of sugared rush, and eats the sagg
And well bestrutted bee's sweet bag ;
Gladding his palate with some store
Of emmets' eggs ; what would he more,
But beards of mice, a newt's stewed thigh,
A bloated earwig, and a fly ;
With the red-capped worm, that's shut
Within the concave of a nut,
Brown as his tooth.   A little moth,
Late fattened in a piece of cloth ;
With withered cherries, mandrake's ears,
Mole's eyes ; to these the slain stag's tears ;
The unctuous dewlaps of a snail,
The broke-heart of a nightingale
O'ercome in music ; with a wine
Ne'er ravished from the flattering vine,
Brought in a dainty daisy, which
He fully quaffs up to bewitch
His blood to height ; this done, commended
Grace by his priest ; the feast is ended.

HERBERT COLE.-1906-

THE GIANT THAT WAS A MILLER

ONCE upon a time there was a Giant that was a miller. He lived in Yorkshire at a place called Dalton. His mill has been rebuilt; but when I was a boy there, the great old building still stood. In front of the house was a long mound, which went by the name of " the Giant's grave," and in the mill was shown a long blade of iron something like a scythe-blade, but not curved, which was the Giant's knife. Now, the Giant who lived at Dalton mill, ground men's bones to make his bread.

Jack seized the moment.

One day he captured a lad called Jack, on Pilmoor, and instead of grinding him body and bones in the mill he kept him as his servant, and never let him get away. Jack served the Giant many years, and never was allowed a holiday. At last he could bear it no longer. Topcliffe fair was coming on, and very hard Jack entreated that he might be allowed to go there to see the lasses and buy some fairings. The Giant surlily refused leave ; but Jack resolved to take it.

The day was hot, and after dinner the Giant lay
down in the mill with his head on a sack and dozed.
He had been eating in the mill, and had laid down a
great loaf of bone bread by his side, and the knife was
in his hand, but his fingers relaxed their hold of it in
sleep.   Jack seized the moment, drew the knife away,
and holding it with both his hands drove the blade into
the single eye of the giant, who woke with a howl of
agony, and starting up barred the door.   Jack thought
he was dead and done for, then ; but he soon found a
way out.   The Giant had a favourite dog, which lay
sleeping in the corner by the fire ; but sprang up when
his master was blinded.   Jack killed the dog with the
fire-tongs, skinned it while his master was getting the
knife out of his eye, and throwing the hide over his
back ran on all-fours barking between the legs of the
Giant, and so escaped.

H . C .

THE PRINCESS OF COLCHESTER

ONG before Arthur and the Knights of the Round Table, there reigned in the eastern part of England a king who kept his Court at Colchester. He was witty, strong, and valiant, by which means he subdued his enemies abroad, and planted peace among his subjects at home. Nevertheless, in the midst of all his glory, his queen died, leaving behind her an only daughter, about fifteen years of age. This little lady, from her courtly carriage, beauty and affability, was the wonder of all that knew her.

But as covetousness is the root of all evil, so it happened here. The king, hearing of a rich dame, who had an only daughter, for the sake of her riches had a mind to marry her; and though she was old, ugly, hook-nosed, and hump-backed, yet all this could not deter him from doing so. Her daughter was a yellow dowdy, full of envy and ill-nature; and, in short, was much of the same mould as her mother. This signified nothing, for in a few weeks the king, attended by the nobility and gentry, brought his new queen home to his palace. She had not been long in the Court before she set the king against his own beautiful daughter, by false reports and evil tales.

The young princess, having lost her father's love, grew weary of the Court, and one day, meeting with her father in the garden, she desired him, with tears in her eyes, to give her a small pittance, and she would go and seek her fortune; to which the king consented, and ordered her mother-in-law to make up a small sum according to her discretion. She went to the queen, who gave her a canvas bag of brown bread and hard cheese, with a bottle of beer; though this was but a very pitiful dowry for a king's daughter.

She took it, returned thanks, and proceeded on her journey, passing through groves, woods, and valleys, till at length she saw an old man sitting on a stone at the mouth of a cave.

"Good morrow, fair maiden," he said, "whither away so fast?"

"Aged father," says she, "I am going to seek my fortune."

"What hast thou in thy bag and bottle?"

"In my bag I have got bread and cheese, and in my bottle good small beer. Will you please to partake of either?"

"Yes," said he, "with all my heart."

With that the lady pulled out her provisions, and bade him eat and welcome.

She saw an old man sitting on a stone at the mouth of a cave.

He did so, and gave her many thanks, and then he said to her : " There is a thick thorny hedge before you, which will appear impassable, but take this wand in your hand, strike three times, and say, ' Pray, hedge, let me come through,' and it will open immediately ; then, a little further, you will find a well ; sit down on the brink of it, and there will come up three golden heads, which will speak ; and whatever they require, that do ! "

Promising she would, she took her leave of him. Coming to the hedge, she pursued the old man's directions ; it opened, and gave her a passage ; then, coming to the well, she had no sooner sat down than a golden head came up singing,—

> " Wash me, and comb me,
> And lay me down softly."

" Yes," said she, and putting forth her hand, with a silver comb performed the office, placing it upon a primrose bank.

Then came up a second and a third head, saying the same as the former. And again she complied, and then pulling out her provisions ate her dinner.

Then said the heads one to another, " What shall we do for this lady who hath used us so kindly ? "

The first said, " I will add such grace to her beauty as shall charm the most powerful prince in the world."

The second said, "I will endow her with fragrance such as shall far exceed the sweetest flowers."

The third said, "My gift shall be none of the least, for, as she is a king's daughter, I'll make her so fortunate that she shall become queen to the greatest prince that reigns."

This done, at their request she let them down into the well again, and so proceeded on her journey.

She had not travelled long before she saw a king hunting in the park with his nobles. She would have shunned him, but the king, having caught a sight of her, approached, and what with her beauty and grace, was so powerfully charmed that he fell in love with her at sight. Forthwith he offered her the finest horse in his train to ride upon; and so, bringing her to his palace, he there caused her to be clothed in the most magnificent manner with white and gold raiment.

This being ended, when the king heard that she was the King of Colchester's daughter he ordered some chariots to be got ready, that he might pay her father a visit. The chariot in which the king and queen rode was adorned with rich ornamental gems of gold. Her father was at first astonished that his daughter had been so fortunate as she was, till the young king made him sensible of all that happened. Great was the joy at Court amongst all, with the exception of the queen and her club-footed daughter, who were ready to burst with malice and envy of her happiness; and the greater was their madness because she was now

above them all. Great rejoicings, with feasting and
dancing, continued many days. Then at length,
with the dowry her father gave her, they returned
home.

The hump-backed sister-in-law, perceiving that
her sister was so happy in seeking her fortune, would
needs do the same; so, disclosing her mind to her
mother, all preparations were made, and she was
furnished not only with rich apparel, but sugar,
almonds, and sweetmeats, in great quantities, and a
large bottle of Malaga sack.

Thus provided, she went the same road as her
sister; and coming near the cave, the old man said,
"Young woman, whither so fast?"

"What is that to you?" said she.

"Then," said he, "what have you in your bag and
bottle?"

She answered, "Good things, which you shall not
be troubled with."

"Won't you give me some?" said he.

"No, not a bit, nor a drop, unless it would choke
you."

The old man frowned, saying, "Evil fortune
attend thee!"

Going on, she came to the hedge, through which
she espied a gap, and thought to pass through it; but,
going in, the hedge closed, and the thorns ran into her
flesh, so that it was with great difficulty that she got
out. Being now in a most sad condition, she searched

for water to wash herself, and looking round, she saw the well.

She sat down on the brink of it, and one of the heads came up, saying, "Wash me, comb me, and lay me down softly." But she banged it with her bottle, saying, "Take this for your washing."

Then the second and third heads came up, and met with no better treatment than the first; whereupon the heads consulted among themselves what evils to plague her with for such usage!

The first said, "Let her be struck with leprosy!"

The second, "Let her hair turn into packthread!"

The third bestowed on her for a husband but a poor country cobbler.

This done, she went on till she came to a town, and it being market-day, the people looked at her, and seeing such a leper's face, all fled but a poor country cobbler. Now, not long before he had mended the shoes of an old hermit, who, having no money, gave him a box of ointment for the cure of the leprosy. So the cobbler, having a mind to do an act of charity, went up to her and asked her who she was?

"I am," said she, "the King of Colchester's daughter-in-law."

"Well," said the cobbler, "if I restore you to your natural complexion, and make a sound cure of you, will you take me for a husband?"

"Yes, friend," replied she; "with all my heart!"

With this the cobbler applied his ointment, and it

worked a cure in a few weeks; after which they were married, and so set forth for the Court at Colchester.

When the queen understood her dear daughter had married nothing but a poor cobbler, she fell into fits of rage, and hanged herself in wrath. The death of the ugly old queen pleased the king, who was glad to be rid of her so soon, and he gave the cobbler a hundred pounds to quit the Court with his lady, and take her to a remote part of the kingdom. There he lived many years mending shoes, his wife spinning thread, and I hope she made him happy.

H. C.

LAZY JACK

A STORY WITHOUT A MORAL

ONCE upon a time there was a boy whose name was Jack, and he lived with his mother upon a dreary common. They were very poor, and the old woman got her living by spinning ; but Jack was so lazy that he would do nothing but bask in the sun in the hot weather, and sit by the corner of the hearth in the winter-time. His mother could not persuade him to do anything for her, and was obliged at last to tell him that if he did not begin to work for his porridge, she would turn him out to get his living as he could.

This threat at length roused Jack, and he went out and hired himself for the day to a farmer for a penny ; but as he was coming home, never having had any money before, he lost it in passing over a brook. "You stupid boy," said his mother, "you should have put it in your pocket." "I'll do so another time," replied Jack.

She dreamt that two fair knights came to her side

Far hae I sought ye, Dear Duke o' Norroway,
Near am I brought to ye; Will ye no turn and speak to me

THE GREEN KNIGHT

~ The Knight was filled with envy at the sight of it .~

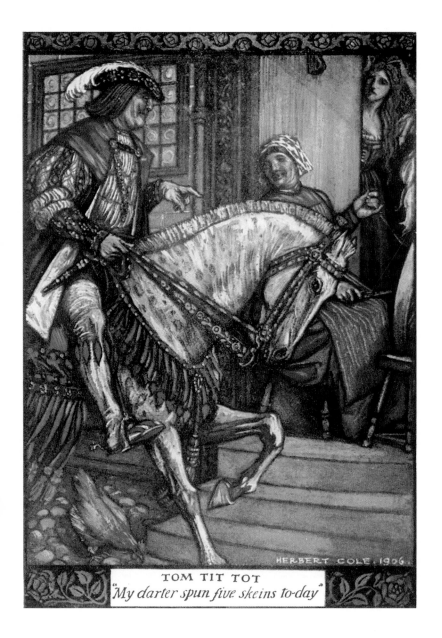

TOM TIT TOT
"My darter spun five skeins to-day"

THE PRINCESS of COLCHESTER

HERBERT COLE 1905

He fell in·a slumbering, and dreamed a marvellous dream.

The next day Jack went out again, and hired himself to a cowkeeper, who gave him a jar of milk for his day's work. Jack took the jar and put it into the large pocket of his jacket, spilling it all long before he got home. "Dear me!" said the old woman, "you should have carried it on your head." "I'll do so another time," replied Jack.

The following day Jack hired himself again to a farmer, who agreed to give him a cream cheese for his services. In the evening Jack took the cheese, and went home with it on his head. By the time he got home the cheese was completely spoilt, part of it being lost and part melted in his hair. "You stupid lout," said his mother, "you should have carried it very carefully in your hands." "I'll do so another time," replied Jack.

The day after this Jack again went out, and hired himself to a baker, who would give him nothing for his work but a large tom cat. Jack took the cat, and began carrying it very carefully in his hands, but in a short time Pussy scratched him so much that he was compelled to let it go. When he got home his mother said to him, "You silly fellow, you should have tied it with a string and dragged it along after you." "I'll do so another time," said Jack.

The next day Jack hired himself to a butcher, who rewarded his labours with a handsome present of a shoulder of mutton. Jack took the mutton, tied it to a string, and trailed it along after him in the dirt, so that by the time he got home the meat was completely spoilt. His mother was this time quite out of patience with him, for the next day was Sunday, and she was obliged to content herself with cabbage for her dinner. "You ninnyhammer," said she to her son, "you should have carried it on your shoulder." "I'll do so another time," replied Jack.

On the Monday Jack went once more, and hired himself to a cattle-keeper, who gave him a donkey for his trouble. Although Jack was very strong, he found some difficulty in hoisting the donkey on his shoulders, but at last he managed it, and began walking home with his prize. Now, it happened that in the course of his journey there lived a rich man with his only daughter, a beautiful girl, but unfortunately deaf and dumb. She had never laughed in her life, and the doctors said she would never recover till somebody made her laugh. Many tried without success, and at last the father, in despair, offered to marry her to the first man who could make her laugh. This young lady happened to be looking out of the window when Jack was passing with the donkey on his shoulders, the legs sticking up in the air, and the sight was so comical and strange, that she burst out into a great fit of laughter, and immediately recovered her speech and hearing. Her father was overjoyed, and fulfilled his promise by marrying her to Jack, who was thus made a rich man for life. They lived in a large house, and Jack's mother lived with them in great happiness until she died.

She burst out into a great fit of laughter ~

❊ ROBIN GOODFELLOW ❊

I

ONCE upon a time, a great while ago, when men
did eat and drink less, and were more honest,
and knew no knavery, there was wont to walk many
harmless spirits called fairies, dancing in brave order in
fairy rings on green hills with sweet music. Sometimes they were invisible, and sometimes took divers
shapes. Many mad pranks would they play, as pinching
of untidy damsels black and blue, and misplacing

things in ill-ordered houses ; but lovingly would they use good girls, giving them silver and other pretty toys, which they would leave for them, sometimes in their shoes, other times in their pockets, sometimes in bright basons and other clean vessels.

Now it chanced that in those happy days, a babe was born in a house to which the fairies did like well to repair. This babe was a boy, and the fairies, to show their pleasure, brought many pretty things thither, coverlets and delicate linen for his cradle ; and capons, woodcock and quail for the christening, at which there was so much good cheer that the clerk had almost forgot to say the babe's name,—Robin Goodfellow. So much for the birth and christening of little Robin.

II

WHEN Robin was grown to six years of age, he was so knavish that all the neighbours did complain of him; for no sooner was his mother's back turned, but he was in one knavish action or other, so that his mother was constrained (to avoid the complaints) to take him with her to market, or wheresoever she went or rode. But this helped little or nothing, for if he rode before her, then would he make mouths and ill-favoured faces at those he met : if he rode behind her, then would he clap his hand on the tail ; so that his mother was weary of the many complaints that came

against him. Yet knew she not how to beat him justly
for it, because she never saw him do that which was
worthy blows. The complaints were daily so renewed
that his mother promised him a whipping. Robin did
not like that cheer, and therefore, to avoid it, he ran
away, and left his mother a-sorrowing for him.

After Robin had travelled a good day's journey
from his mother's house he sat down, and being weary
he fell asleep. No sooner had slumber closed his eyelids, but he thought he saw many goodly proper
little personages in antic measures tripping about him,
and withal he heard such music, as he thought that
Orpheus, that famous Greek fiddler (had he been alive),
compared to one of these had been but a poor muscian.
As delights commonly last not long, so did those end
sooner than Robin would willingly they should have
done; and for very grief he awaked, and found by him
lying a scroll wherein was written these lines following
in golden letters,—

" Robin, my only son and heir,
How to live take thou no care :
By nature thou hast cunning shifts,
Which I'll increase with other gifts.
Wish what thou wilt, thou shall it have ;
And for to fetch both fool and knave,
Thou hast the power to change thy shape,
To horse, to hog, to dog, to ape.
Transformed thus, by any means
See none thou harm'st but knaves and queanes :
But love thou those that honest be,
And help them in necessity.

Do thus and all the world shall know
The pranks of Robin Goodfellow,
For by that name thou called shall be
To age's last posterity ;
And if thou keep my just command,
One day thou shall see Fairy Land ! "

Robin, having read this, was very joyful, yet longed
he to know whether he had the power or not, and to
try it he wished for some meat ; presently a fine dish
of roast veal was before him. Then wished he for
plum-pudding ; he straightway had it. This liked
him well, and because he was weary, he wished himself
a horse : no sooner was his wish ended, but he was
changed into as fine a nag as you need see, and
leaped and curveted as nimbly as if he had been in
stable at rack and manger a full month. Then he
wished himself a black dog, and he was so ; then a
green tree, and he was so. So from one thing to
another, till he was quite sure that he could change
himself to anything whatsoever he liked.

Thereupon full of delight at his new powers,
Robin Goodfellow set out, eager to put them to the
test.

As he was crossing a field, he met with a red-faced
carter's clown, and called to him to stop.

" Friend," quoth he, " what is a clock ? "

" A thing," answered the clown, " that shows the
time of the day."

" Why then," said Robin Goodfellow, " be thou
a clock and tell me what time of the day it is."

"I owe thee not so much service," answered the clown again, "but because thou shalt think thyself beholden to me, know that it is the same time of the day as it was yesterday at this time!"

These shrewd answers vexed Robin Goodfellow, so that in himself he vowed to be revenged of the clown, which he did in this manner.

Robin Goodfellow turned himself into a bird, and followed this fellow who was going into a field a little from that place to catch a horse that was at grass. The horse being wild ran over dyke and hedge, and the fellow after, but to little purpose, for the horse was too swift for him. Robin was glad of this occasion, for now or never was the time to have his revenge.

Presently Robin shaped himself exactly like the horse that the clown followed, and so stood right before him. Then the clown took hold of the horse's mane and got on his back, but he had not ridden far when, with a stumble, Robin hurled his rider over his head, so that he almost broke his neck. But then again he stood still, and let the clown mount him once more.

By the way which the clown now would ride was a great pond of water of a good depth, which covered the road. No sooner did he ride into the very middle of the pond, than Robin Goodfellow turned himself into a fish, and so left him with nothing but the pack-saddle on which he was riding betwixt his legs. Meanwhile the fish swiftly swam to the bank. And then Robin, changed to a naughty boy again, ran away laughing, " *Ho, ho, hoh*," leaving the poor clown half drowned and covered with mud.

III

As Robin took his way then along a green hedge-side he fell to singing,—

> " And can the doctor make sick men well ?
> And can the gipsy a fortune tell
> Without lily, germander, and cockle-shell ?
> With sweet-brier,
> And bon-fire
> And straw-berry wine,
> And columbine.
>
> When Saturn did live, the sun did shine,
> The king and the beggar on roots did dine,
> With lily, germander, and sops in wine.
> With sweet-brier,
> And bon-fire,
> And straw-berry wine,
> And columbine."

And when he had sung this over, he fell to wondering what he should next turn himself into. Then as he saw the smoke rise from the chimneys of the next town, he thought to himself, it would be to him great sport to walk the streets with a broom on his shoulder, and cry " Chimney sweep."

But when presently Robin did this, and one did call him, then did Robin run away laughing, " *Ho, ho, hoh !* "

Next he set about to counterfeit a lame beggar,—begging very pitifully, but when a stout chandler came out of his shop to give Robin an alms, again he skipped off nimbly, laughing, as his naughty manner was.

That same night, he did knock at many men's doors, and when the servants came out, he blew out their candle and straightway vanished in the dark street, with his "*Ho, ho, hoh !*"

All these mirthful tricks did Robin play, that day and night, and in these humours of his he had many pretty songs, one of which I will sing as perfect as I can. He sang it in his chimney-sweeper's humour to the tune of, " *I have been a fiddler these fifteen years.*"

> "Black I am from head to foot,
>   And all doth come by chimney soot.
> Then, maidens, come and cherish him
>   That makes your chimneys neat and trim."

But it befell that, on the very next night to his playing the chimney-sweep, Robin had a summons from the land where there are no chimneys.

For King Oberon, seeing Robin Goodfellow do so many merry tricks, called him out of his bed with these words, saying,—

> " Robin, my son, come quickly rise:
>   First stretch, then yawn, and rub your eyes;
> For thou must go with me to-night,
>   And taste of Fairy-land's delight."

Robin, hearing this, rose and went to him. There

were with King Oberon many fairies, all attired in green. All these, with King Oberon, did welcome Robin Goodfellow into their company. Oberon took Robin by the hand and led him a fair dance : their musician had an excellent bag-pipe made of a wren's quill and the skin of a Greenland fly. This pipe was so shrill, and so sweet, that a Scottish pipe compared to it, it would no more come near it than a Jew's-harp doth to an Irish harp. After they had danced, King Oberon said to Robin,—

> " Whene'er you hear the piper blow,
> Round and round the fairies go !
> And nightly you must with us dance,
> In meadows where the moonbeams glance,
> And make the circle, hand in hand—
> That is the law of Fairy-land !
> There thou shalt see what no man knows ;
> While sleep the eyes of men doth close !

So marched they, with their piper before, to the Fairy Land. There did King Oberon show Robin Goodfellow many secrets, which he never did open to the world. And there, in Fairy Land, doth Robin Goodfellow abide now this many a long year.

TOM HICKATHRIFT

 **L**ONG before William the Conqueror, there dwelt a man in the Isle of Ely, named Thomas Hickathrift, a poor labouring man, but so strong that he was able to do in one day the ordinary work of two. He had an only son, whom he christened Thomas, after his own name. The old man put his son to good learning, but he would take none, for he was none of the wisest, but something soft, and had no docility at all in him. God calling this good man, the father, to his rest, his mother, being tender of him, kept him by her hard labour as well as she could ; but this was no easy matter, for Tom would sit all day in the chimney-corner, instead of doing anything to help her, and although at the time we are speaking of he was only ten years old, he would eat more than four or five ordinary men, and was five feet and a half in height, and two feet and a half broad. His hand was more like a shoulder of mutton than a boy's hand, and he

was altogether like a little monster ; but yet his great strength was not known.

Tom's strength came to be known in this manner : his mother, it seems, as well as himself, for they lived in the days of merry old England, slept upon straw. Now, being a tidy old creature, she must every now and then have a new bed, and one day having been promised a bottle of straw by a neighbouring farmer, after much begging, she got her son to fetch it. Tom, however, made her borrow a cart-rope first, before he would budge a step, without saying what he wanted it for ; but the poor woman, too glad to gain his help upon any terms, let him have it at once. Tom, swinging the rope round his shoulders, went to the farmer's, and found him with two men threshing in a barn. Having told what he wanted, the farmer said he might take as much straw as he could carry. Tom at once took him at his word, and, placing the rope in a right position, rapidly made up a bundle containing at least a cartload, the men jeering at him all the while. Their merriment, however, did not last long, for Tom flung the enormous bundle over his shoulders, and walked away with it without any difficulty, and left them all gaping after him.

After this exploit Tom was no longer allowed to be idle. Every one tried to secure his services, and we are told many tales of his mighty strength. On one occasion, having been offered as great a bundle of fire-wood as he could carry, he marched off with one of the largest trees in the forest. Tom was also extremely fond of attending fairs; and in cudgelling, wrestling, or throwing the hammer, there was no one who could compete with him. He thought nothing of flinging a huge hammer into the middle of a river a mile off, and, in fact, performed such extraordinary feats, that the folk began to have a fear of him.

At length a brewer at Lynn, who required a strong lusty fellow to carry his beer to the Marsh and to Wisbeach, after much persuasion, and promising him a new suit of clothes and as much as he liked to eat and drink, secured Tom for his business. The distance he daily travelled with the beer was upwards of twenty miles, for although there was a shorter cut through the Marsh, no one durst go that way for fear of a monstrous giant, who was lord of a portion of the district, and who killed or made slaves of every one he could lay his hands upon.

Now, in the course of time, Tom was thoroughly tired of going such a roundabout way, and without telling his plans to any one, he resolved to pass through the giant's domain, or lose his life in the attempt. This was a bold undertaking, but good living had so increased Tom's strength and courage, that venturesome as he was before, his hardiness was so much increased that he would have faced a still greater danger. He accordingly drove his cart in the forbidden direction, flinging the gates wide open, as if for the purpose of making his daring more plain to be seen.

At length he was espied by the giant, who was in a
rage at his boldness, but consoled himself by thinking
that Tom and the beer would soon become his prey.
"Sirrah," said the monster, "who gave you permission
to come this way ? Do you not know how I make all
stand in fear of me ? and you, like an impudent rogue,
must come and fling my gates open at your pleasure !
Are you careless of your life ? Do not you care what
you do ? But I will make you an example for all
rogues under the sun ! Dost thou not see how many
thousand heads hang upon yonder tree—heads of those
who have offended against my laws ? But thy head shall
hang higher than all the rest for an example ! " But
Tom made him answer : " A dishclout in your teeth
for your news, for you shall not find me to be one of
them." "No ! " said the giant, in astonishment and
indignation ; "and what a fool you must be if you
come to fight with such a one as I am, and bring never
a weapon to defend yourself ! " Quoth Tom, "I have
a weapon here that will make you know you are a
traitorly rogue." This speech highly incensed the giant,
who immediately ran to his cave for his club, intending
to dash out Tom's brains at one blow. Tom was now
much distressed for a weapon, as by some chance he
had forgot one, and he began to reflect how very little
his whip would help him against a monster twelve feet
in height and six feet round the waist. But while
the giant was gone for his club, Tom bethought himself, and turning his cart upside down, adroitly takes

He was amazed to see the weapons.

out the axletree, which would serve him for a staff, and removing a wheel, fits it to his arm instead of a shield— very good weapons indeed in time of trouble, and worthy of Tom's wit. When the monster returned with his club, he was amazed to see the weapons with which Tom had armed himself; but uttering a word of defiance, he bore down upon the poor fellow with such heavy strokes that it was as much as Tom could do to defend himself with his wheel. Tom, however, at length cut the giant a heavy blow with the axle-tree on the side of his head, that he nearly reeled over. "What!" said Tom, "have you drunk of my strong beer already?" This inquiry did not, as we may suppose, mollify the giant, who laid on his blows so sharply and heavily that Tom was obliged to defend himself. By-and-bye, not making any impression on the wheel, he got almost tired out, and was obliged to ask Tom if he would let him drink a little, and then he would fight again. "No," said Tom, "my mother did not teach me that wit : who would be fool then?" The end may readily be imagined ; Tom having beaten the giant, cut off his head, and entered the cave, which he found completely filled with gold and silver.

The news of this victory rapidly spread throughout the country, for the giant had been a common enemy to the people about. They made bonfires for joy, and showed their respect to Tom by every means in their power. A few days afterwards Tom took possession of the cave and all the giant's treasure. He pulled

down the former, and built a magnificent house on the
spot ; but as for the land stolen by the giant, part of it
he gave to the poor for their common, merely keeping
enough for himself and his good old mother, Jane
Hickathrift.

Tom was now a great man and a hero with all the
country folk, so that when any one was in danger or
difficulty, it was to Tom Hickathrift he must turn.
It chanced that about this time many idle and rebellious
persons drew themselves together in and about the Isle of
Ely, and set themselves to defy the King and all his men.

By this time, you must know, Tom Hickathrift had
secured to himself a trusty friend and comrade, almost
his equal in strength and courage, for though he was
but a tinker, yet he was a great and lusty one. Now
the sheriff of the county came to Tom, under cover of
night, full of fear and trembling, and begged his aid
and protection against the rebels, " else " said he, " we
be all dead men ! " Tom, nothing loth, called his friend
the tinker, and as soon as it was day, led by the sheriff,
they went out armed with their clubs to the place where
the rebels were gathered together. When they were
got thither, Tom and the tinker marched up to the
leaders of the band, and asked them why they were set
upon breaking the King's peace. To this they answered
loudly, " Our will is our law, and by that alone we will
be governed ! " " Nay," quoth Tom, "if it be so,
these trusty clubs are our weapons, and by them alone
you shall be chastised." These words were no sooner

uttered than they madly rushed on the throng of men, bearing all before them, and laying twenty or thirty sprawling with every blow. The tinker struck off heads with such violence that they flew like balls for miles about, and when Tom had slain hundreds and so broken his trusty club, he laid hold of a lusty raw-boned miller and made use of him as a weapon till he had quite cleared the field.

If Tom Hickathrift had been a hero before, he was twice a hero now. When the King heard of it all, he sent for him to be knighted, and when he was Sir Thomas Hickathrift nothing would serve him but that he must be married to a great lady of the county.

So married he was, and a fine wedding they had of it. There was a great feast given, to which all the poor widows for miles round were invited, because of Tom's mother, and rich and poor feasted together. Among the poor widows who came was an old woman called Stumbelup, who with much ingratitude stole from the great table a silver tankard. But she had not got safe away before she was caught and the people were so enraged at her wickedness that they had nearly hanged her. However, Sir Tom had her rescued, and commanded that she should be drawn on a wheel-barrow through the streets and lanes of Cambridge, holding a placard in her hand on which was written—

> "I am the naughty Stumbelup,
> Who tried to steal the silver cup."

THE THREE BEARS

ONCE upon a time there were Three Bears, who
lived together in a house of their own, in a
wood. One of them was a Little, Small, Wee Bear;
and one was a Middle-sized Bear, and the other was a
Great, Huge Bear. They had each a pot for their
porridge; a little pot for the Little, Small, Wee Bear;
and a middle-sized pot for the Middle Bear; and a
great pot for the Great, Huge Bear. And they had
each a chair to sit in; a little chair for the Little,
Small, Wee Bear; and a middle-sized chair for the

Middle Bear ; and a great chair for the Great, Huge Bear. And they had each a bed to sleep in ; a little bed for the Little, Small, Wee Bear ; and a middle-sized bed for the Middle Bear ; and a great bed for the Great, Huge Bear.

One day, after they had made the porridge for their breakfast, and poured it into their porridge-pots, they walked out into the wood while the porridge was was cooling, that they might not burn their mouths, by beginning too soon to eat it. And while they were walking, a little old Woman came to the house. She could not have been a good, honest old Woman ; for first she looked in at the window, and then she peeped in at the keyhole ; and seeing nobody in the house, she lifted the latch. The door was not fastened, because the Bears were good Bears, who did nobody any harm, and never suspected that anybody would harm them. So the little old Woman opened the door, and went in ; and well pleased she was when she saw the porridge on the table. If she had been a good little old Woman, she would have waited till the Bears came home ; and then, perhaps, they would have asked her to breakfast ; for they were good Bears,—a little rough or so, as the manners of Bears are, but for all that very good-natured and hospitable. But she was an impudent, bad old Woman, and set about helping herself.

So first she tasted the porridge of the Great, Huge Bear, and that was too hot for her ; and she said a bad word about that. And then she tasted the porridge of the Middle Bear, and that was too cold for her ; and she said a bad word about that too. And then she went to the porridge of the Little, Small, Wee Bear, and tasted that ; and that was neither too hot, nor too cold, but just right ; and she liked it so well, that she ate it all up : but the naughty old Woman said a bad word about the little porridge-pot, because it did not hold enough for her.

Then the little old Woman sate down in the chair of the Great, Huge Bear, and that was too hard for her. And then she sate down in the chair of the Middle Bear, and that was too soft for her. And then she sate down in the chair of the Little, Small Wee Bear, and that was neither too hard, nor too soft, but just right. So she seated herself in it, and there she sate till the bottom of the chair came out, and down came she plump upon the ground. And the naughty old Woman said a wicked word about that too.

Then the little old Woman went upstairs into the bed-chamber in which the three Bears slept. And first she lay down upon the bed of the Great, Huge Bear ; but that was too high at the head for her. And next she lay down upon the bed of the Middle Bear ; and that was too high at the foot for her. And then she lay down upon the bed of the Little, Small, Wee Bear ; and that was neither too high at the head, nor at the foot, but just right. So she covered herself up comfortably, and lay there till she fell fast asleep.

The little old woman sits down in the Little Bear's chair.

By this time the Three Bears thought their porridge would be cool enough ; so they came home to breakfast. Now the little old Woman had left the spoon of the Great, Huge Bear standing in his porridge.

"Somebody has been at my porridge!"

said the Great, Huge Bear, in his great, rough, gruff voice. And when the Middle Bear looked at his, he saw that the spoon was standing in it too. They were wooden spoons; if they had been silver ones, the naughty old Woman would have put them in her pocket.

"SOMEBODY HAS BEEN AT MY PORRIDGE!"

said the Middle Bear, in his middle voice.

Then the Little, Small, Wee Bear looked at his. and there was the spoon in the porridge-pot, but the porridge was all gone.

"*Somebody has been at my porridge, and has eaten it all up!*"

said the, Little, Small, Wee Bear, in his little, small, wee voice.

Upon this the Three Bears, seeing that some one had entered their house, and eaten up the Little, Small, Wee Bear's breakfast, began to look about them. Now the little old Woman had not put the hard cushion straight when she rose from the chair of the Great, Huge Bear.

"Somebody has been sitting in my chair!"

said the Great, Huge Bear, in his great rough, gruff voice.

And the little old Woman had squatted down the soft cushion of the Middle Bear.

"SOMEBODY HAS BEEN SITTING IN MY CHAIR!"

said the Middle Bear in his middle voice.

And you know what the little old Woman had done to the third chair.

" Somebody has been sitting in my chair, and has sate the bottom of it out ! "

said the Little, Small, Wee Bear, in his little, small, wee voice.

Then the Three Bears thought it necessary that they should make farther search ; so they went upstairs into their bed-chamber. Now the little old Woman had pulled the pillow of the Great, Huge Bear out of its place.

"Somebody has been lying in my bed!"

said the Great, Huge Bear, in his great, rough, gruff voice.

And the little old Woman had pulled the bolster of the Middle Bear out of its place.

" SOMEBODY HAS BEEN LYING IN MY BED ! "

said the Middle Bear, in his middle voice.

And when the Little, Small, Wee Bear came to look at his bed, there was the bolster in its place ; and the pillow in its place upon the bolster ; and upon the pillow was the little old Woman's ugly, dirty head,— which was not in its place, for she had no business there.

" Somebody has been lying in my bed, and here she is ! "

said the Little, Small, Wee Bear, in his little, small, wee voice.

The little old Woman had heard in her sleep the great, rough, gruff voice of the Great, Huge Bear; but she was so fast asleep that it was no more to her than the roaring of wind, or the rumbling of thunder. And she had heard the middle voice of the Middle Bear, but it was only as if she had heard some one speaking in a dream. But when she heard the Little, Small, Wee Bear, it was so sharp, and so shrill, that it awakened her at once. Up she started; and when she saw the Three Bears on one side of the bed, she tumbled herself out at the other, and ran to the window. Now the window was open, because the Bears, like good, tidy Bears, as they were, always opened their bed-chamber window when they got up in the morning. Out the little old Woman jumped; and whether she broke her neck in the fall; or ran into the wood and was lost there; or found her way out of the wood, and was taken up by the constable and sent to the House of Correction for a vagrant as she was, I cannot tell. But the Three Bears never saw anything more of her.

THE HISTORY OF TOM THUMB.

I T is said that in the days of the famed Prince Arthur, who was king of Britain, in the year 516 there lived a great magician, called Merlin, the most learned and skilful enchanter in the world at that time.

This great magician, who could assume any form he pleased, was travelling in

153

the disguise of a poor beggar, and being very much fatigued, he stopped at the cottage of an honest plough-man to rest himself, and asked for some refreshment.

The countryman gave him a hearty welcome, and his wife, who was a very good-hearted, hospitable woman, soon brought him some milk in a wooden bowl, and some coarse brown bread on a platter.

Merlin was much pleased with this homely repast and the kindness of the ploughman and his wife ; but he could not help seeing that though everything was neat and comfortable in the cottage, they seemed both to be sad and much cast down. He therefore questioned them on the cause of their sadness, and learned that they were miserable because they had no children.

The poor woman declared, with tears in her eyes, that she should be the happiest creature in the world if she had a son ; and although he was no bigger than her husband's thumb, she would be satisfied.

Merlin was so much amused with the idea of a boy no bigger than a man's thumb, that he made up his mind to pay a visit to the queen of the fairies, and ask her to grant the poor woman's wish. The droll fancy of such a little person among the human race pleased the fairy queen too, greatly, and she promised Merlin that the wish should be granted. Accordingly, in a short time after, the ploughman's wife had a son, who, wonderful to relate, was not a bit bigger than his father's thumb.

The fairy queen, wishing to see the little fellow

thus born into the world, came in at the window while the mother was sitting up in bed admiring him. The queen kissed the child, and giving it the name of Tom Thumb, sent for some of the fairies, who dressed her little favourite as she bade them.

> "An oak-leaf hat he had for his crown ;
> His shirt of web by spiders spun ;
> With jacket wove of thistle's down ;
> His trowsers were of feather's done.
> His stockings, of apple-rind, they tie
> With eyelash from his mother's eye :
> His shoes were made of mouse's skin,
> Tann'd with the downy hair within."

It is remarkable that Tom never grew any larger than his father's thumb, which was only of an ordinary size ; but as he got older he became very cunning and full of tricks. When he was old enough to play with the boys, and had lost all his own cherry-stones, he used to creep into the bags of his playfellows, fill his pockets, and, getting out unseen, would again join in the game.

One day, however, as he was coming out of a bag of cherry-stones, where he had been pilfering as usual, the boy to whom it belonged chanced to see him. "Ah, ha! my little Tommy," said the boy, "so I have caught you stealing my cherry-stones at last, and you shall be rewarded for your thievish tricks." On saying this, he drew the string tight round his neck, and gave the bag such a hearty shake, that poor little Tom's legs, thighs, and body were sadly bruised. He

roared out with pain, and begged to be let out, promising never to be guilty of such bad practices again.

A short time afterwards his mother was making a
batter-pudding, and Tom being very anxious to see
how it was made, climbed up to the edge of the bowl ;
but unfortunately his foot slipped and he plumped
over head and ears into the batter, unseen by his
mother, who stirred him into the pudding-bag, and
put him in the pot to boil.

The batter had filled Tom's mouth, and prevented
him from crying ; but, on feeling the hot water, he
kicked and struggled so much in the pot, that his
mother thought that the pudding was bewitched, and,
instantly pulling it out of the pot, she threw it to the
door. A poor tinker, who was passing by, lifted up
the pudding, and, putting it into his budget, he then
walked off. As Tom had now got his mouth cleared
of the batter, he then began to cry aloud, which so
frightened the tinker that he flung down the pudding
and ran away. The pudding being broke to pieces by
the fall, Tom crept out covered over with the batter,
and with difficulty walked home. His mother, who
was very sorry to see her darling in such a woful state,
put him into a tea-cup, and soon washed off the batter ;
after which she kisssd him, and laid him in bed.

Soon after the adventure of the pudding, Tom's
mother went to milk her cow in the meadow, and she
took him along with her. As the wind was very high,
fearing lest he should be blown away, she tied him to

a thistle with a piece of fine thread. The cow soon saw the oak-leaf hat, and, liking the look of it, took poor Tom and the thistle at one mouthful. While the cow was chewing the thistle Tom was afraid of her great teeth, which threatened to crush him in pieces, and he roared out as loud as he could : "Mother, mother !"

"Where are you, Tommy, my dear Tommy?" said his mother.

"Here, mother," replied he, "in the cow's mouth."

His mother began to cry and wring her hands; but the cow, surprised at the odd noise in her throat, opened her mouth and let Tom drop out. Fortunately his mother caught him in her apron as he was falling to the ground, or he would have been dreadfully hurt. She then put Tom in her bosom and ran home with him.

Tom's father made him a whip of a barley straw to drive the cattle with, and having one day gone into the fields, he slipped a foot and rolled into the furrow. A raven, which was flying over, picked him up, and flew with him to the top of a giant's castle that was near the sea-side, and there left him.

Tom was in a dreadful state, and did not know what to do; but he was soon more dreadfully frightened; for old Grumbo the giant came up to walk on the terrace, and seeing Tom, he took him up and swallowed him like a pill.

The giant had no sooner swallowed Tom than he began to repent what he had done; for Tom began to kick and jump about so much that he felt very uncom-

fortable, and at last threw him up again into the sea.
A large fish swallowed Tom the moment he fell into
the sea, which was soon after caught, and bought for
the table of King Arthur. When they opened the fish
in order to cook it, everyone was astonished at finding
such a little boy, and Tom was quite delighted to be
out again. They carried him to the king, who made
Tom his dwarf, and he soon grew a great favourite at
Court; for by his tricks and gambols he not only
amused the king and queen, but also all the knights of
the Round Table.

It is said that when the king rode out on horseback,
he often took Tom along with him, and if a shower
came on, he used to creep into his majesty's waistcoat
pocket, where he slept till the rain was over.

King Arthur one day asked Tom about his parents,
wishing to know if they were as small as he was, and
whether rich or poor. Tom told the king that his
father and mother were as tall as any of the sons about
Court, but rather poor. On hearing this, the king
carried Tom to his treasury, the place where he kept
all his money, and told him to take as much money as
he could carry home to his parents, which made the
poor little fellow caper with joy. Tom went immediately to fetch a purse, which was made of a water-
bubble, and then returned to the treasury, where he
got a silver threepenny-piece to put into it.

Our little hero had some trouble in lifting the
burden upon his back; but he at last succeeded in

getting it placed to his mind, and set forward on his journey. However, without meeting with any accident and after resting himself more than a hundred times by the way, in two days and two nights he reached his father's house in safety.

Tom had travelled forty-eight hours with a huge silver-piece on his back, and was almost tired to death, when his mother ran out to meet him, and carried him into the house.

Tom's parents were both happy to see him, and the more so as he had brought such an amazing sum of money with him ; but the poor little fellow was excessively wearied, having travelled half a mile in forty-eight hours, with a huge silver threepenny-piece on his back. His mother, in order to recover him, placed him in a walnut shell by the fireside, and feasted him for three days on a hazel-nut, which made him very sick ; for a whole nut used to serve him a month.

Tom was soon well again ; but as there had been a fall of rain, and the ground was very wet, he could not travel back to King Arthur's Court ; therefore his mother, one day when the wind was blowing in that direction, made a little parasol of cambric paper, and tying Tom to it, she gave him a puff into the air with her mouth, which soon carried him to the king's palace.

Just at the time when Tom came flying across the courtyard, the cook happened to be passing with the king's great bowl of furmenty, which was a dish his majesty was very fond of ; but unfortunately the poor little fellow fell plump into the middle of it, and splashed the hot furmenty about the cook's face.

The cook, who was an ill-natured fellow, being in a terrible rage at Tom for frightening and scalding him with the furmenty, went straight to the king, and said that Tom had jumped into the royal furmenty, and thrown it down out of mere mischief. The king was so enraged when he heard this, that he ordered Tom to be seized and tried for high treason ; and there being no person who dared to plead for him, he was condemned to be beheaded immediately.

On hearing this dreadful sentence pronounced, poor Tom fell a-trembling with fear, but, seeing no means of escape, and observing a miller close to him gaping with his great mouth, as country boobies do at a fair, he took a leap, and fairly jumped down his throat. This exploit was done with such activity that not one person present saw it, and even the miller did not know the trick which Tom had played upon him. Now, as Tom had disappeared, the court broke up, and the miller went home to his mill.

When Tom heard the mill at work he knew he was clear of the court, and therefore he began to roll and tumble about, so that the poor miller could get no rest, thinking he was bewitched ; so he sent for a doctor. When the doctor came, Tom began to dance and sing ; and the doctor, being as much frightened as the miller, sent in haste for five other doctors and twenty learned men.

When they were debating about this extraordinary case, the miller happened to yawn, when Tom, seizing the chance, made another jump, and alighted safely upon his feet on the middle of the table.

The miller, who was very much provoked at being tormented by such a little pigmy creature, fell into a terrible rage, and, laying hold of Tom, ran to the king with him ; but his majesty, being engaged with state affairs, ordered him to be taken away, and kept in custody till he sent for him.

The cook was determined that Tom should not slip out of his hands this time, so he put him into a mouse-trap, and left him to peep through the wires. Tom had remained in the trap a whole week, when he was sent for by King Arthur, who pardoned him for throwing down the furmenty, and took him again into favour.   On account of his wonderful feats of activity, Tom was knighted by the king, and went under the name of the renowned Sir Thomas Thumb.   As Tom's clothes had suffered much in the batter-pudding, the furmenty, and the insides of the giant, miller, and fishes, his majesty ordered him a new suit of clothes, and to be mounted as a knight.

> " Of Butterfly's wings his shirt was made,
>   His boots of chicken's hide ;
> And by a nimble fairy blade,
> Well learned in the tailoring trade,
>   His clothing was supplied.—
> A needle dangled by his side ;
> A dapper mouse he used to ride,
> Thus strutted Tom in stately pride ! "

It was certainly very diverting to see Tom in this dress, and mounted on the mouse, as he rode out a-hunting with the king and nobility, who were all ready to expire with laughter at Tom and his fine prancing charger.

One day, as they were riding by a farmhouse, a large cat, which was lurking about the door, made a spring, and seized both Tom and his mouse. She then ran up a tree with them, and was beginning to devour the mouse; but Tom boldly drew his sword, and attacked the cat so fiercely that she let them both fall, when one of the nobles caught him in his hat, and laid him on a bed of down, in a little ivory cabinet.

The queen of the fairies came soon after to pay Tom a visit, and carried him back to Fairy-land, where he lived several years. During his residence there, King Arthur, and all the persons who knew Tom, had died; and as he was desirous of being again at Court, the fairy queen, after dressing him in a suit of clothes, sent him flying through the air to the palace, in the days of King Thunstone, the successor of Arthur. Every one flocked round to see him, and being carried to the king, he was asked who he was—whence he came— and where he lived? Tom answered,—

> "My name is Tom Thumb,
> From the fairies I've come.
> When King Arthur shone,
> His Court was my home.
> In me he delighted,
> By him I was knighted;
> Did you never hear of Sir Thomas Thumb?"

The king was so charmed with this address that he ordered a little chair to be made, in order that Tom might sit upon his table, and also a palace of gold, a span high, with a door an inch wide, to live in. He also gave him a coach, drawn by six small mice.

The queen was so enraged at the honour paid to Sir Thomas that she resolved to ruin him, and told the king that the little knight had been saucy to her.

The king sent for Tom in great haste, but being fully aware of the danger of royal anger, he crept into an empty snail-shell, where he lay for a long time, until he was almost starved with hunger; but at last he ventured to peep out, and seeing a fine large butterfly on the ground, near his hiding-place, he approached very cautiously, and getting himself placed astride on it, was immediately carried up into the air. The butterfly flew with him from tree to tree and from field to field, and at last returned to the Court, where the king and nobility all strove to catch him; but at last poor Tom fell from his seat into a watering-pot, in which he was almost drowned.

When the queen saw him she was in a rage, and said he should be beheaded; and he was again put into a mouse-trap until the time of his execution.

However, a cat, observing something alive in the trap, patted it about till the wires broke, and set Thomas at liberty.

The king received Tom again into favour, which

he did not live to enjoy, for a large spider one day attacked him ; and although he drew his sword and fought well, yet the spider's poisonous breath at last overcame him ;

> " He fell dead on the ground where he stood,
>   And the spider suck'd every drop of his blood."

King Thunstone and his whole Court were so sorry at the loss of their little favourite, that they went into mourning, and raised a fine white marble monument over his grave, with the following epitaph :—

> " Here lyes Tom Thumb, King Arthur's knight,
>   Who died by a spider's cruel bite,
>   He was well known in Arthur's Court,
>   Where he afforded gallant sport ;
>   He rode at tilt and tournament,
>   And on a mouse a-hunting went.
>   Alive he filled the Court with mirth ;
>   His death to sorrow soon gave birth.
>   Wipe, wipe your eyes, and shake your head
>   And cry,—Alas ! Tom Thumb is dead ! "

THE GIANT OF SAINT MICHAEL'S

WHEN King Arthur was king of this realm, it befell at one time that he departed and entered into the sea at Sandwich with all his army, with a great multitude of ships, galleys, and dromons,[1] sailing on the sea.

And as the king lay in his cabin in the ship, he fell in a slumbering, and dreamed a marvellous dream:

---

[1] War-vessels, with high prows.

him seemed that a dreadful dragon did drown much of his people, and he came flying out of the west, and his head was enamelled with azure, and his shoulders shone as gold, his body like mails [1] of a marvellous hue, his tail full of tatters, his feet full of fine sable, and his claws like fine gold ; and an hideous flame of fire flew out of his mouth, like as the land and water had flamed all of fire. After him, there came out of the Orient a grimly boar, all black, sailing in a cloud, and his paws as big as a post. He was rugged looking, roughly ; he was the foulest beast that ever man saw, he roared and romed [2] so hideously that it was marvel to hear. Then the dreadful dragon advanced him, and came in the wind like a falcon, giving great strokes on the boar, and the boar hit him again with his grisly tusks that his breast was all bloody, and that the hot blood made all the sea red of his blood. Then the dragon flew away all on an height, and came down with such a swough, and smote the boar on the ridge, which was ten foot large from the foot to the tail, and smote the boar all to powder, both flesh and bones, that it flittered all abroad on the sea. And therewith the king awoke anon and was sore abashed of this dream ; and sent anon for a wise man, commanding to tell him the meaning of his dream.

"Sir," said the wise man, "the dragon that thou dreamedst of betokeneth thine own person that sailest here, and the colour of his wings be thy realms that

[1] A coat of mail.   [2] Growled.

thou hast won, and his tail which is all to-tattered signifieth the noble knights of the Round Table. And the boar that the dragon slew coming from the clouds, either betokeneth some tyrant that tormenteth the people, or else that thou art like to fight with some giant thyself, being horrible and abominable, whose peer ye saw never in your days. Wherefore of this dreadful dream doubt thee nothing, but as a conqueror come forth thyself."

Then after this soon they had sight of land, and when they were there, a husbandman of that country came and told him there was a great giant which had slain, murdered, and devoured much people of the country, and had been sustained seven year with the children of the commons of that land, insomuch, that all the children be all slain and destroyed.

"And now late," saith this countryman, "he hath taken the Duchess of Brittany as she rode with her train, and hath led her to his lodging which is in a mountain, for to keep her to her life's end ; and many people followed her, more than five hundred, but all they might not rescue her, but they left her shrieking and crying lamentably, wherefore I suppose that he hath slain her. Now as thou art a rightful king have pity on this lady, and revenge us all as thou art a noble conqueror."

"Alas !" said King Arthur, "this is a great mischief, I had rather than the best realm that I have that I had been a furlong way tofore him, for to have rescued that lady. Canst thou bring me where this giant haunteth?"

"Yea, sir," said the good man, "lo, yonder where as thou seest those two great fires, there thou shalt find him, and more treasure than I suppose is in all France."

When the king had understood this piteous case he returned into his tent.

Then he called unto him Sir Kay and Sir Bedivere, and commanded them secretly to make ready horse and harness for himself and them twain, for after evensong he would ride on pilgrimage with them two only unto Saint Michael's Mount. And then anon he made him ready and armed him at all points, and took his horse and his shield. And so they three departed thence, and rode forth as fast as ever they might till that they came unto the foot of that mount. And there they alighted, and the king commanded them to tarry there, for he would himself go into that mount. And so he ascended up into that hill till he came to a great fire, and there he found a careful widow wringing her hands and making great sorrow, sitting by a grave new made.

King Arthur saluted her, and demanded of her wherefore she made such lamentation: to whom she answered and said, "Sir knight, speak soft, for yonder is a demon: if he hear thee speak he will come and destroy thee; I hold thee unhappy; what dost thou here in this mountain? for if ye were such

The giant sat at supper.

fifty as ye be, ye were not able to make resistance against this devil : here lieth a duchess dead, the which was the fairest of all the world, wife to Sir Howell, Duke of Brittany ; he hath murdered her."

"Dame," said the king, "I come from the noble conqueror King Arthur, for to treat with that tyrant for his liege people."

"Fie upon such treaties," said the widow, "he setteth not by the king, nor by no man else. Beware, approach him not too nigh, for he hath vanquished fifteen kings, and hath made him a coat full of precious stones, embroidered with their beards, which they sent him to have his love for salvation of their people at this last Christmas. And if thou wilt, speak with him at yonder great fire at supper."

"Well," said Arthur, "I will accomplish my message for all your fearful words."

And he went forth by the crest of that hill, and saw where the giant sat at supper gnawing on a limb of a man, baking his broad limbs by the fire, and three fair damsels turning three spits, whereon were broached twelve young children like young birds.

When King Arthur beheld that piteous sight he had great compassion on them so that his heart bled for sorrow, and hailed him saying in this wise,—

"He that all the world wieldeth, give thee short life and shameful death. Why hast thou murdered these young innocent children, and murdered this duchess? Therefore arise and dress thee, thou glutton; for this day shalt thou die of my hand."

Then the glutton anon started up and took a great club in his hand, and smote at the king that his coronal fell to the ground. And the king hit the giant again, and carved his body till his blood fell down in two streams. Then the giant threw away his club, and caught the king in his arms that he crushed his ribs. Then the three maidens kneeled down and called to Christ for help and comfort of Arthur. And then Arthur weltered and wrestled with the giant, that he was other while under and another time above. And so weltering and wallowing they rolled down the hill till they came to the sea mark, and ever as they so weltered Arthur smote him with his dagger, and it fortuned they came to the place where as the two knights were that kept Arthur's horse. Then when they saw the king fast in the giant's arms they came and loosed him.

And then the king commanded Sir Kay to smite off the giant's head, and to set it upon a truncheon of a spear, and bear it to Sir Howell, and tell him that his enemy was slain. "After this," said the king, "let his head be bound to a barbican that all the people may see and behold it; and go ye two up to the mountain and fetch me my shield, my sword, and the club of iron. And as for the treasure take ye it, for ye shall find there goods out of number. So I have the kirtle and the club, I desire no more. This was the fiercest giant that ever I met with, save one in the mount of Arabe which I overcame, but this was greater and fiercer."

Then the knights fetched the club and the kirtle, and some of the treasure they took to themselves, and returned again to the host. And anon this was known through all the country, wherefore the people came and thanked the king. And he said again, "Give the thanks to God, and part the goods among you." And after that, King Arthur said and commanded his cousin Howell that he should ordain for a church to be builded on the same hill, in the worship of Saint Michael.

H· C

THE FAIRIES' FROLIC

Human Characters :—Mopso, Joculo, and Frisio.

Enter Fairies, singing and dancing.

FAIRY SONG.

By the moon we sport and play,
With the night begins our day ;
As we dance the dew doth fall—
Trip it, little urchins all,
Lightly as the little bee,
Two by two, and three by three ;
And about go we, and about go we.

Jo. What mawmets [1] are these ?
Fris. O they be the fairies that haunt these woods.
Mop. O we shall be pinched most cruelly !
1st Fai. Will you have any music, sir ?
2d Fai. Will you have any fine music ?
3d Fai. Most dainty music ?

[1] Dolls, puppets.

174

Mop. We must set a face on it now ; there is no
    flying.
No, sir, we very much thank you.
  1st Fai. O but you shall, sir.
  Fris. No, I pray you, save your labour.
  2d Fai. O, sir ! it shall not cost you a penny.
  Jo. Where be your fiddles ?
  3d Fai. You shall have most dainty instruments, sir ?
  Mop. I pray you, what might I call you?
  1st Fai. My name is Penny.
  Mop. I am sorry I cannot purse you.
  Fris. I pray you, sir, what might I call you ?
  2d Fai. My name is Cricket.
  Fris. I would I were a chimney for your sake.
  Jo. I pray you, you pretty little fellow, what's your
    name ?
  3d Fai. My name is little little Puck.
  Jo. Little little Puck?   O you are a dangerous fairie !
I care not whose hand I were in, so I were out of
    yours.
  1st Fai. I do come about the cops,
        Leaping upon flowers' tops ;
        Then I get upon a fly,
        She carries me about the sky,
        And trip and go.
  2d Fai. When a dew-drop falleth down,
        And doth light upon my crown,
        Then I shake my head and skip,
        And about I trip.

3d Fai. When I see a girl asleep,
   Underneath her curls I peep,
   There to sport, and there I play,
   When she wakes, I run away.

Jo. I thought where I should have you.

1st Fai. Will 't please you dance, sir?

Jo. Indeed, sir, I cannot handle my legs.

2d Fai. O you must needs dance and sing.
   Which if you refuse to do,
   We will pinch you black and blue;
   And about we go.

FAIRIES sing.

Round about, round about, in a fine ring a,
Thus we dance, thus we dance, and thus we sing a;
Trip and go, to and fro, over this green a,
All about, in and out, for our brave queen a.

Round about, round about, in a fine ring a,
Thus we dance, thus we dance, and thus we sing a
Trip and go, to and fro, over this green a,
All about, in and out, for our brave queen a.

We have danced round about, in a fine ring a,
We have danced lustily, and thus we sing a;
All about, in and out, over this green a,
To and fro, trip and go, to our brave queen a.

JACK AND THE BEAN-STALK

THERE once lived a poor widow, in a cottage which stood in a country village, a long distance from London, for many years.

The widow had only a child named Jack, whom she gratified in everything ; the end of her foolish kindness was, that Jack paid little attention to anything she said ; and he was heedless and naughty. His follies were not owing to bad nature, but to his mother never having chided him. As she was not rich, and he would not work, she was obliged to support herself and him by selling everything she had. At last nothing remained, only a cow.

The widow, with tears in her eyes, could not help scolding Jack. "Oh ! you wicked boy," said she, "by your naughty course of life you have now brought us both to fall ! Heedless, heedless boy ! I have not money enough to buy a bit of bread for another day : nothing remains but my poor cow, and that must be sold, or we must starve !"

Jack was in a degree of tenderness for a few minutes, but soon over ; and then becoming very hungry for want of food he teased his poor mother to let him sell the cow ; which at last she sadly allowed him to do.

As he went on his journey he met a butcher, who asked why he was driving the cow from home ? Jack replied he was going to sell it. The butcher had some wonderful beans, of different colours, in his bag, which caught Jack's fancy. This the butcher saw, who, knowing Jack's easy temper, made up his mind to take advantage of it, and offered all the beans for the cow. The foolish boy thought it a great offer. The bargain was momently struck, and the cow exchanged for a few paltry beans. When Jack hastened home with the beans and told his mother, and showed them to her, she kicked the beans away in a great passion. They flew in all directions, and fell as far as the garden.

Early in the morning Jack arose from his bed, and seeing something strange from the window, he hastened downstairs into the garden, where he soon found that some of the beans had taken root, and sprung up wonderfully : the stalks grew of an immense thickness, and had so entwined, that they formed a ladder like a chain in view.

Looking upwards, he could not descry the top, it seemed to be lost in the clouds. He tried it, found it firm, and not to be shaken. A new idea immediately struck him : he would climb the bean-stalk, and see whither it would lead. Full of this plan, which made him forget even his hunger, Jack hastened to tell it to his mother.

He at once set out, and after climbing for some hours, reached the top of the bean-stalk, tired and almost exhausted. Looking round, he was surprised to find himself in a strange country ; it seemed to be quite a barren desert ; not a tree, shrub, house, or living creature was to be seen.

Jack sat himself pensively upon a block of stone, and thought of his mother ; his hunger attacked him, and now he felt sorrowful for his disobedience in climbing the bean-stalk against her will ; and made up his mind that he must now die for want of food.

However, he walked on, hoping to see a house where he might beg something to eat. Suddenly he saw a beautiful young woman at some distance. She was dressed in an elegant manner, and had a small white wand in her hand, on the top of which was a peacock of pure gold. She came near and said : " I will tell to you a story your mother dare not. But before I begin, I require a solemn promise on your part to do what I command. I am a fairy, and unless you perform exactly what I direct you to do, you will take from me the power to assist you ; and there is little doubt but that you will die in the attempt." Jack was rather frightened at this caution, but promised to follow her directions.

" Your father was a rich man, with a greatly generous nature. It was his practice never to refuse help to the poor people about him ; but, on the contrary, to seek out the helpless and distressed. Not many miles from your father's house lived a huge giant, who was the dread of the country around for cruelty and wickedness. This creature was moreover of a very envious spirit, and disliked to hear others talked of for their goodness and humanity, and he vowed to do him a mischief, so that he might no longer hear his good actions made the subject of everyone's talk. Your father was too good a man to fear evil from others ; so it was not long before the cruel giant found a chance to put his wicked threats into practice ; for hearing that your parents were about passing a few days with a friend at some distance from home, he caused your father to be waylaid and murdered, and your mother to be seized on their way homeward.

"At the time this happened, you were but a few months old. Your poor mother, almost dead with affright and horror, was borne away by the cruel giant's servants, to a dungeon under his house, in which she and her poor babe were both long kept prisoners. Distracted at the absence of your parents, the servants went in search of them ; but no tidings of either could be got. Meantime he caused a will to be found making over all your father's property to him as your guardian, and as such he took open possession.

"After your mother had been some months in prison, the giant offered to restore her to liberty, on condition that she would solemnly swear that she

~ Jack easily found his way to the bean-stalk and came down ~

would never tell the story of her wrongs to any one. To put it out of her power to do him any harm, should she break her oath, the giant had her put on ship-board, and taken to a distant country ; where she was left with no more money for her support than what she got by selling a few jewels she had hidden in her dress.

"I was appointed your father's guardian at his birth ; but fairies have laws to which they are subject as well as mortals. A short time before the giant killed your father, I transgressed ; my punishment was the loss of my power for a certain time, which, alas, entirely prevented my helping your father, even when I most wished to do so. The day on which you met the butcher, as you went to sell your mother's cow, my power was restored. It was I who secretly prompted you to take the beans in exchange for the cow. By my power the bean-stalk grew to so great a height, and formed a ladder. The giant lives in this country ; you are the person who must punish him for all his wickedness. You will meet with dangers and difficulties, but you must persevere in avenging the death of your father, or you will not prosper in any of your doings.

"As to the giant's goods, everything he has is yours, though you are deprived of it ; you may take, therefore, what part of it you can. You must, how-ever, be careful, for such is his love for gold, that the first loss he discovers will make him outrageous and very watchful for the future. But you must still pursue him ; for it is only by cunning that you can

ever hope to get the better of him, and become possessed of your rightful property, and the means of
justice overtaking him for his barbarous murder. One
thing I desire is, do not let your mother know you are
aware of your father's history till you see me again.

"Go along the direct road; you will soon see the
house where your cruel enemy lives. While you do
as I order you, I will protect and guard you; but
remember, if you disobey my commands, a dreadful
punishment awaits you."

As soon as she had made an end she disappeared,
leaving Jack to follow his journey. He walked on
till after sunset, when, to his great joy, he espied a
large mansion. This pleasant sight revived his droop-
ing spirits; he redoubled his speed, and reached it
shortly. A well-looking woman stood at the door:
he spoke to her, begging she would give him a morsel
of bread and a night's lodging. She expressed the
greatest surprise at seeing him; and said it was quite
uncommon to see any strange creature near their house,
for it was mostly known that her husband was a very
cruel and powerful giant, and one that would eat
human flesh, if he could possibly get it.

This account terrified Jack greatly, but still, not for-
getting the fairy's protection, he hoped to elude the giant,
and therefore he begged the woman to take him in for
one night only, and hide him where she thought proper.
The good woman at last suffered herself to be persuaded,
for she had a kind heart, and at last led him into the house.

First they passed an elegant hall, finely furnished; they then went through several spacious rooms, all in the same style of grandeur, but they seemed to be quite forsaken and desolate. A long gallery came next; it was very dark, just large enough to show that, instead of a wall each side, there was a grating of iron, which parted off a dismal dungeon, from whence issued the groans of several poor victims whom the cruel giant kept shut up in readiness for his very large appetite. Poor Jack was in a dreadful fright at witnessing such a horrible scene, which caused him to fear that he would never see his mother, but be captured lastly for the giant's meat; but still he recollected the fairy, and a gleam of hope forced itself into his heart.

The good woman then took Jack to a large kitchen, where a great fire was kept; she bade him sit down, and gave him plenty to eat and drink. When he had done his meal and enjoyed himself, he was disturbed by a hard knocking at the gate, so loud as to cause the house to shake. Jack was hidden in the oven, and the giant's wife ran to let in her husband.

Jack heard him accost her in a voice like thunder, saying: "Wife! wife! I smell fresh meat!" "Oh! my dear," replied she, "it is nothing but the people in the dungeon." The giant seemed to believe her, and at last seated himself by the fireside, whilst the wife prepared supper.

By degrees Jack managed to look at the monster through a small crevice. He was much surprised to

see what an amazing quantity he devoured, and sup-
posed he would never have done eating and drinking.
After his supper was ended, a very curious hen was
brought and placed on the table before him. Jack's
curiosity was great to see what would happen. He
saw that it stood quiet before him, and every time the
giant said : " Lay!" the hen laid an egg of solid gold.
The giant amused himself a long time with his hen ;
meanwhile his wife went to bed. At length he fell
asleep, and snored like the roaring of a cannon.
Jack, finding him still asleep at daybreak, crept softly
from his hiding-place, seized the hen, and ran off with
her as fast as his legs could possibly carry him.

Jack easily found his way to the bean-stalk, and
came down better and quicker than he expected. His
mother was overjoyed to see him. " Now, mother,"
said Jack, "I have brought you home that which will
make you rich." The hen laid as many golden eggs
as they desired ; they sold them, and soon had as much
riches as they wanted.

For a few months Jack and his mother lived very
happy, but he longed to pay the giant another visit.
Early one morning he again climbed the bean-stalk,
and reached the giant's mansion late in the evening :
the woman was at the door as before. Jack told her
a pitiful tale, and prayed for a night's shelter. She
told him that she had admitted a poor hungry boy
once before, and the little ingrate had stolen one of the
giant's treasures, and ever since that she had been

cruelly used. She however led him to the kitchen,
gave him a supper, and put him in a lumber closet.
Soon after the giant came in, took his supper, and
ordered his wife to bring down his bags of gold and
silver. Jack peeped out of his hiding-place, and
observed the giant counting over his treasures, and
after which he carefully put them in bags again, fell
asleep, and snored as before. Jack crept quietly from
his hiding-place, and approached the giant, when a little
dog under the chair barked furiously. Much to his
surprise, the giant slept on soundly, and the dog
ceased. Jack seized the bags, reached the door in
safety, and soon arrived at the bottom of the bean-
stalk. When he reached his mother's cottage, he
found it quite deserted. Full of astonishment he ran
into the village, and an old woman directed him to a
house, where he found his mother apparently dying.
On being told of our hero's safe return, his mother
revived and soon recovered. Jack then presented two
bags of gold and silver to her.

His mother saw that something preyed upon his
mind heavily, and tried to find out the cause ; but
Jack knew too well what the consequence would be
should he discover the cause of his melancholy to her.
He did his utmost therefore to conquer the great
desire which now forced itself upon him in spite of himself for another journey up the bean-stalk, but in vain.

On the longest day Jack arose as soon as it was
light, climbed the bean-stalk, and reached the top with

some little trouble.   He found the road, journey, etc.,
the same as before.   He arrived at the giant's house in
the evening, and found his wife standing as usual at
the door.   Jack now appeared a different character,
and had disguised himself so completely that she did
not appear to remember him.   However, when he
begged admittance, he found it very difficult to persuade her.   At last he prevailed, was allowed to go in,
and was hidden in the copper.

When the giant returned, he said, as usual:
" Wife! wife! I smell fresh meat!"   But Jack felt
quite composed, as he had said so before, and had soon
been satisfied.   However, the giant started up
suddenly, and notwithstanding all his wife could say,
he searched all round the room.   Whilst this was going
forward, Jack was much terrified, and ready to die with
fear, wishing himself at home a thousand times; but
when the giant approached the copper, and put his hand
upon the lid, Jack thought his death was certain.   Fortunately the giant ended his search there, without moving
the lid, and seated himself quietly by the fireside.

When the giant's supper was over, he commanded
his wife to fetch down his harp.   Jack peeped under
the copper-lid, and soon saw the most beautiful one
that could be imagined.   It was put by the giant on
the table, who said: "Play," and it instantly played
of its own accord.   The music was uncommonly fine.
Jack was delighted, and felt more anxious to get the harp
into his possession than either of the former treasures.

The giant's soul was not attuned to harmony, and the music soon lulled him into a sound sleep. Now, therefore, was the time to carry off the harp, as the giant appeared to be in a more profound sleep than usual. Jack soon made up his mind, got out of the copper, and seized the harp; which, however, being enchanted by a fairy, called out loudly: "Master, master!"

The giant awoke, stood up, and tried to pursue Jack; but he had drank so much that he could not stand. Jack ran as quick as he could. In a little time the giant was well enough to walk slowly, or rather to reel after him. Had he been sober, he must have overtaken Jack instantly; but as he then was, Jack contrived to be first at the top of the bean-stalk. The giant called to him all the way along the road in a voice like thunder, and was sometimes very near to him.

The moment Jack got down the bean-stalk, he called out for a hatchet: one was brought him directly. Just at that instant the giant began to descend, but Jack with his hatchet cut the bean-stalk close off at the root, and the giant fell headlong into the garden. The fall instantly killed him.

Jack heartily begged his mother's pardon for all the sorrow and affliction he had caused her, promising most faithfully to be dutiful and obedient to her in future. He proved as good as his word, and became a pattern of affectionate behaviour for the rest of her life; and, let us hope, he never lost his mother-wit.

QUEEN MAB'S GOOD GRACE

IF ye will with Mab find grace,
　　Set each platter in his place ;
Rake the fire up, and get
Water in, ere sun be set,
Wash your pails and cleanse your dairies,
Sluts are loathsome to the fairies ;
Sweep your house ; who doth not so,
Mab will pinch her by the toe.

He bought a camel and went into the country of PRESTER-JOHN
who rides on a white elephant and has Kings to wait upon him.

OLD FORTUNATUS

FAR from here in the famous isle of Cyprus there
is a stately city called Famagosta. There, a
long time ago, lived one Theodorus, descended of
noble parents, who left him with a great estate. But
being brought up to nothing but idleness, he soon
wasted the greater half of his riches to the great grief
of his relations, who, thinking to make him leave these
courses, determined to match him to a rich merchant's
daughter in the city of Nicovia, named Graciana.

Now for a time, Theodorus was content to lead a quiet life, and Graciana brought her husband a fine little son, who was named Fortunatus. So one would think nothing could have kept Theodorus from being the most happy person in the world. But this was not long the case ; for when he had enjoyed these things for some time, he grew tired of them, and began to keep company with young noblemen of the Court, and in a few years spent all his fortune. He was now very sorry for what he had done, but it was too late ; and there was nothing he could do, but to work at some trade to support his wife and child. For all this Graciana never found fault with him, but still loved her husband the same as before, saying,—

"Dear Theodorus, to be sure I do not know how to work at any trade ; but if I cannot help you in earning money, I will help you to save it."

So Theodorus set to work ; and though the Lady Graciana had always been used only to ring her bell for everything that she wanted, she now scoured the kettles and washed the clothes with her own hands.

They went on in this manner till Fortunatus was sixteen years of age. When that time came, one day, as they were all sitting at dinner, Theodorus fixed his eyes on his son, and sighed deeply.

"What is the matter with you, father?" said Fortunatus.

"Ah ! my child," said Theodorus, " I have reason enough to be sorry, when I think of the noble fortune which I have spent, and that my folly will force you to labour for your living."

"Father," replied Fortunatus, "do not grieve about it. I have often thought that it was time I should do something for myself; and though I have not been brought up to any trade, yet I hope I can contrive to support myself somehow."

When Fortunatus had done his dinner, he took his hat and walked to the sea-side, thinking of what he could do, so as to be no longer a burden to his parents. Just as he reached the sea-shore, the Earl of Flanders, who had been to Jerusalem, was embarking on board his ship with all his servants, to set sail for Flanders. Fortunatus now thought he would offer himself to be the Earl's page. When the Earl saw that he was a smart-looking lad, and heard the quick replies which he made to his questions, he took him into his service; so at once they all went on board. On their way the ship stopped a short time at the port of Venice, where Fortunatus saw many strange things, which made him wish still more to travel, and taught him much that he did not know before.

Soon after they came to Flanders; and they had not been long on shore, before the Earl, his master, was married to the daughter of the Duke of Cleves. The wedding was kept with all sorts of public feasting, and games on horseback called tilts, which lasted many days; and, among the rest, the Earl's lady gave two jewels as prizes to be played for, each of them the value of a hundred crowns. One of them was won by Fortunatus, and the other by Timothy, a servant of the Duke of Burgundy; who afterwards ran another tilt with Fortunatus, so that the winner was to have both the jewels. So they tilted, and, at the fourth course, Fortunatus hoisted Timothy a full spear's length from his horse, and thus won both the jewels; which pleased the Earl and Countess so much that they praised Fortunatus, and thought better of him than ever. At this time, also, Fortunatus had many rich presents given him by the lords and ladies of the Court. But the high favour shown him made his fellow-servants jealous; and one, named Robert, who had always pretended a great friendship for Fortunatus, made him believe that for all his seeming kindness, the Earl in secret envied him his great skill in tilting. Robert said, too, that he had heard the Earl give private orders to one of his servants to find some way of killing him next day, while they should all be out hunting.

Fortunatus thanked the wicked Robert for what he thought a great kindness; and the next day, at day-break, he took the swiftest horse in the Earl's stables, and left the country. When the Earl heard that Fortunatus had gone away in a hurry, he was much surprised, and asked all his servants what they knew about the matter; but they all denied knowing any-thing of it, or why he had left them. The Earl then said: "Fortunatus was a lad for whom I had a great esteem; I am sure some of you must have given him an affront; if I discover it, I shall not fail to punish the guilty person." In the meantime Fortunatus, when he found himself out of the Earl's country, stopped at an inn to refresh himself, and began to reckon how much he had about him. He took out all his fine clothes and jewels, and could not help putting them on. He then looked at himself in the glass, and thought that, to be sure, he was quite a fine smart fellow. Next he took out his purse, and counted the money that had been given him by the lords and ladies of the Earl's court. He found that in all he had five hundred crowns; so he bought a horse, and took care to send back the one that he had taken from the Earl's stable.

He then set off for Calais, crossed the Channel, landed safely at Dover, and went on to London, where he soon made his way into genteel company, and had once the honour to dance with the daughter of a duke at the lord mayor's ball. This sort of life, as anybody may well think, soon made away with his little stock of money. When Fortunatus found that he had not a penny left, he began to think of going back again to France; and soon after went on board a ship bound to Picardy. He landed in that country; but finding no employment he set off for Brittany, when he lost his way in crossing a wood, and was forced to stay in it all night. The next morning he was little better off, for he could find no path. So he

walked about from one part of the wood to another,
till at last, on the evening of the second day, he saw a
spring, at which he drank very heartily ; but still he
had nothing to eat, and was ready to die with hunger.
When night came on, he heard the growling of wild
beasts, so he climbed up a high tree for safety ; and
he had hardly seated himself in it, before a lion walked
fiercely up to the spring to drink. This made him
very much afraid. When the lion had gone away, a
bear came to drink also ; and, as the moon shone very
bright, the beast looked up, and saw Fortunatus, and
straightway began to climb up the tree to get at him.

Fortunatus drew his sword, and sat quiet till the
bear was come within arm's length ; and then he ran
him through the body. This drove the bear so very
savage, that he made a great spring to get at him ;
the bough broke, and down he fell, and lay sprawling
and howling on the ground. Fortunatus now looked
around on all sides ; and as he saw no more wild
beasts near, he thought this would be a good time to
ger rid of the bear at once ; so down he came, and
killed him at a single blow. Being almost starved for
want of food, the poor youth stooped down, and was
going to suck the blood of the bear ; but looking
round once more, to see if any wild beast were coming,
he on a sudden beheld a beautiful lady standing by his
side, with a bandage over her eyes, leaning upon a
wheel, and looking as if she were going to speak,
which she soon did, in these words : " Know, young

man, that my name is Fortune ; I have the power to
bestow wisdom, strength, riches, health, beauty, and
long life : one of these I am willing to grant you—
choose for yourself which it shall be."

Fortunatus was not a moment before he answered :
"Good lady, I wish to have riches in such plenty that
I may never again know what it is to be so hungry as
I now find myself." The lady then gave him a purse,
and told him that in all the countries where he might
happen to be, he need only put his hand into the purse
as often as he pleased, and he would be sure to find in
it ten pieces of gold ; that the purse should never fail
of yielding the same sum as long as it was kept by him
and his children ; but that when he and his children
should be dead, then the purse would lose its power.

Fortunatus now did not know what to do with
himself for joy, and began to thank the lady very
much ; but she told him that he had better think of
making his way out of the wood. She then directed
him which path to take, and bade him farewell. He
walked by the light of the moon, as fast as his weak-
ness and fatigue would let him, till he came near an
inn. But before he went into it, he thought it would
be best to see whether the Lady Fortune had been as
good as her word ; so he put his hand into his purse,
and to his great joy he counted ten pieces of gold.
Having nothing to fear, Fortunatus walked boldly up
to the inn, and called for the best supper they could
get ready in a minute ; "For," said he, "I must wait

till to-morrow before I am very nice. I am so hungry now, that almost anything will do." Fortunatus very soon ate quite enough, and then called for every sort of wine in the house, and drank his fill. After supper, he began to think what sort of life he should lead ; " For," said he to himself, " I shall now have money enough for everything I can desire." He slept that night in the very best bed in the house ; and the next day he ordered the finest victuals of all kinds. When he rang his bell, all the waiters tried who should run fastest, to ask him what he pleased to want ; and the landlord himself, hearing what a noble guest was come to his house, took care to be standing at the door to bow to him when he should be passing out.

Fortunatus asked the landlord whether any fine horses could be got near at hand ; also, if he knew of some smart-looking, clever men-servants who wanted places. By chance the landlord was able to provide him with both. As he had now got everything he wanted, he set out on the finest horse that was ever seen, with two servants, for the nearest town. There he bought some grand suits of clothes, put his two servants into liveries laced with gold, and then went on to Paris. Here he took the best house that was to be had, and lived in great pomp. He invited the nobility, and gave grand balls to all the most beautiful ladies of the Court. He went to all public places of amusement, and the first lords in the country invited him to their houses. He had lived in this manner for about a year,

The Lady then gave him a purse

when he began to think of going to Famagosta to visit
his parents, whom he had left very poor. "But,"
thought Fortunatus, "as I am young and have not
seen much of the world, I should like to meet with
some person of more knowledge than I have, who
would make my journey both useful and pleasing to
me." Soon after this he met with an old gentleman,
called Loch-Fitty, who was a native of Scotland, and
had left a wife and ten children a great many years ago,
in hopes to better his fortune ; but now, owing to
many accidents, was poorer than ever, and had not
money enough to take him back to his family.

When Loch-Fitty found how much Fortunatus
wished to obtain knowledge, he told him many of the
strange adventures he had met with, and gave him an
account of all the countries he had been in, as well as
of the customs, dress, and manners of the people.
Fortunatus thought to himself, " This is the very man
I stand in need of ; " so at once he made him a good
offer, which the old gentleman agreed to, but made the
bargain that he might first go and visit his family.
Fortunatus told him that he should. " And," said he,
" as I am a little tired of being always in the midst of
such noisy pleasures as we find at Paris, I will, with
your leave, go with you to Scotland, and see your wife
and children." They set out the very next day, and
came safe to the house of Loch-Fitty ; and in all the
journey, Fortunatus did not once wish to change his
kind companion for all the pleasures and grandeur he

had left behind. Loch-Fitty kissed his wife and
children, five of whom were daughters, and the most
beautiful creatures that were ever beheld. When they
were seated, his wife said to him : "Ah! dear Lord
Loch-Fitty, how happy I am to see you once again!
Now I hope we shall enjoy each other's company for
the rest of our lives. What though we are poor!
We will be content if you will but promise not to
think of leaving us again to get riches, only because
we have a noble title."

Fortunatus heard this with great surprise.
'What!'" said he, "are you a lord? Then you shall
be a rich lord too. And that you may not think I lay
you under any burden in the fortune I shall give you,
I will put it in your power to make me your debtor
instead. Give me your youngest daughter, Cassandra,
for a wife, and accompany us as far as Famagosta, and
take all your family with you, that you may have
pleasant company on your way back, when you have
rested in that place from your fatigue."

Lord Loch-Fitty shed some tears of joy to think
he should at last see his family again raised to all the
honours which it had once enjoyed. He gladly agreed
to the marriage of Fortunatus with his daughter
Cassandra, and then told him the reasons that had
forced him to drop his title and live poor at Paris.
When Lord Loch-Fitty had ended his story, they
agreed that the very next morning the Lady Cassandra
should be asked to accept the hand of Fortunatus ; and

that, if she should consent, they would set sail in a few days for Famagosta. The next morning the offer was made to her, as had been agreed on ; and Fortunatus had the pleasure of hearing from the lips of the beautiful Cassandra, that the very first time she cast her eyes on him she thought him the most handsome gentleman in the world.

Everything was soon ready for them to set out on the journey. Fortunatus, Lord Loch-Fitty, his lady, and their ten children, then set sail in a large ship : they had a good voyage, and landed safe at the port of Famagosta. There, however, Fortunatus found, with great grief and self-reproach, that his father and mother were both dead. However, as he was an easy-tempered gentleman, and had his betrothed Cassandra and her whole family to reconcile him to his grief, it did not last very long ; the wedding took place almost immediately ; so they lived all together in Famagosta, and in very great style. By the end of the first year, the Lady Cassandra had a little son, who was christened Ampedo ; and the next year another, who was christened Andolucia. For twelve years Fortunatus lived a very happy life with his wife and children, and his wife's kindred ; and as each of her sisters had a fortune given her from the purse of Fortunatus, they soon married very well. But by this time he began to long to travel again ; and he thought, as he was now so much older and wiser than when he was at Paris, he might go by himself, for Lord Loch-Fitty was at this

time too old to bear fatigue. After he had, with great
trouble, got the consent of the Lady Cassandra, and
made her a promise to stay away only two years, he
made all things ready for his journey ; and taking his
lady into one of his private rooms, he showed her
three chests of gold. He told her to keep one of these
for herself, and take charge of the other two for their
sons, in case any evil should happen to him. He then
led her back to the room where the whole family were
sitting, embraced them all tenderly one by one, and set
sail with a fair wind for Alexandria.

When Fortunatus came to this place, he was told it
was the custom to make a handsome present to the
sultan ; so he sent him a piece of plate that cost five
thousand pounds. The sultan was so much pleased
with this, that he ordered a hundred casks of spices to
be given to Fortunatus in return. Fortunatus sent
these straight to the Lady Cassandra, with the most
tender letters, by the same ship that brought him,
which was then going back to Famagosta. Having
stated that he wished to travel through his country by
land, he obtained from the sultan such passports and
letters as he might stand in need of, to the other
princes in those parts. He then bought a camel, hired
proper servants, and set off on his travels. He went
through Turkey, Persia, and from thence to Carthage ;
he next went into the country of Prester John, who
rides upon a white elephant, and has kings to wait on
him. Fortunatus made him some rich presents, and

went on to Calcutta ; and, in coming back, he took
Jerusalem in the way, and so came again to Alexandria,
where he had the good fortune to find the same ship
that had brought him, and to learn from the captain
that his wife and family were all in perfect health.
The first thing he did was to pay a visit to his old
friend the sultan, to whom he again made a handsome
present, and was invited to dine at his palace. After
dinner, the sultan said : " It must be vastly amusing,
Fortunatus, to hear an account of all the places you
have seen ; pray favour me with a history of your
travels." Fortunatus did as he was desired, and
pleased the sultan very much by telling him the many
odd adventures he had met with ; and, above all, the
manner of his first becoming known to the Lord Loch-
Fitty, and the desire of that lord to maintain the
honours of his family. When he had ended, the
sultan said he was greatly pleased with what he had
heard, but that he possessed a more curious thing than
any Fortunatus had told him of. He then led him
into a room almost filled with jewels, opened a large
closet, and took out a cap, which he said was of greater
value than all the rest. Fortunatus thought the
sultan was joking, and told him he had seen many
a better cap than that. "Ah !" said the sultan,
"that is because you do not know its value. Whoever puts this cap on his head, and wishes to be in
any part of the world, will find himself there in a
moment."

"Indeed!" said Fortunatus; "and pray, is the man living who made it?"

"I know nothing about that," said the sultan.

"One would hardly believe it," said Fortunatus. "Pray, sir, is it very heavy?"

"Not at all," replied the sultan; "you may feel it."

Fortunatus took up the cap, put it on his head, and could not help wishing himself on board the ship that was going back to Famagosta. In less than a moment he was carried on board of her, just as she was ready to sail; and there being a brisk gale, they were out of sight in half an hour, before the sultan had even time to repent of his folly for letting Fortunatus try the cap on his head. The ship came safe to Famagosta, after a happy passage, and Fortunatus found his wife and children well; but Lord Loch-Fitty and his lady had died of old age, and were buried in the same grave.

Fortunatus now began to take great pleasure in teaching his two boys all sorts of useful learning, and also such manly sports as wrestling and tilting. Now and then he thought about the curious cap which had brought him home, and then would wish he could just take a peep at what was passing in other countries; which wish was always fulfilled: but he never stayed there more than an hour or two, so that the Lady Cassandra did not miss him, and was no longer made uneasy by his love of travelling.

At last, Fortunatus began to grow old, and the Lady Cassandra fell sick and died. The loss of her caused him so much grief, that soon after he fell sick too. As he thought he had not long to live, he called his two sons to his bedside, and told them the secrets of the purse and the cap, which he begged they would not, on any account, make known to others. "Follow my example," said he : "I have had the purse these forty years, and no living person knew from what source I obtained my riches." He then told them to make use of the purse between them, and to live together in friendship ; and embracing them, died soon after. Fortunatus was buried with great pomp by the side of Lady Cassandra, in his own chapel, and was for a long time mourned by the people of Famagosta.

DICK
WHITTINGTON
AND HIS
CAT

IN the reign of the famous King Edward III. there was a little boy called Dick Whittington, whose father and mother died when he was very young, so that he remembered nothing at all about them, and was left a ragged little fellow, running about a country village. As poor Dick was not old enough to work, he was very

badly off; he got but little for his dinner, and sometimes nothing at all for his breakfast ; for the people
who lived in the village were very poor indeed, and
could not spare him much more than the parings of
potatoes, and now and then a hard crust of bread.

For all this Dick Whittington was a very sharp
boy, and was always listening to what everybody
talked about. On Sunday he was sure to get near the
farmers, as they sat talking on the tombstones in the
churchyard, before the parson was come ; and once a
week you might see little Dick leaning against the
sign-post of the village alehouse, where people stopped
to drink as they came from the next market town ;
and when the barber's shop door was open, Dick listened
to all the news that his customers told one another.

In this manner Dick heard a great many very
strange things about the great city called London ; for
the foolish country people at that time thought that
folks in London were all fine gentlemen and ladies ;
and that there was singing and music there all day
long ; and that the streets were all paved with gold.

One day a large waggon and eight horses, all with
bells at their heads, drove through the village while
Dick was standing by the sign-post. He thought that
this waggon must be going to the fine town of London ;
so he took courage, and asked the waggoner to let him
walk with him by the side of the waggon. As soon as
the waggoner heard that poor Dick had no father or
mother, and saw by his ragged clothes that he could

not be worse off than he was, he told him he might go if he would, so they set off together.

I could never find out how little Dick contrived to get meat and drink on the road; nor how he could walk so far, for it was a long way; nor what he did at night for a place to lie down to sleep in. Perhaps some good-natured people in the towns that he passed through, when they saw he was a poor little ragged boy, gave him something to eat; and perhaps the waggoner let him get into the waggon at night, and take a nap upon one of the boxes or large parcels in the waggon.

Dick, however, got safe to London, and was in such a hurry to see the fine streets paved all over with gold, that I am afraid he did not even stay to thank the kind waggoner; but ran off as fast as his legs would carry him, through many of the streets, thinking every moment to come to those that were paved with gold; for Dick had seen a guinea three times in his own little village, and remembered what a deal of money it brought in change; so he thought he had nothing to do but to take up some little bits of the pavement, and should then have as much money as he could wish for.

Poor Dick ran till he was tired, and had quite forgot his friend the waggoner; but at last, finding it grow dark, and that every way he turned he saw nothing but dirt instead of gold, he sat down in a dark corner and cried himself to sleep.

Little Dick was all night in the streets; and next

morning, being very hungry, he got up and walked about, and asked everybody he met to give him a halfpenny to keep him from starving; but nobody stayed to answer him, and only two or three gave him a halfpenny; so that the poor boy was soon quite weak and faint for the want of victuals.

At last a good-natured looking gentleman saw how hungry he looked. "Why don't you go to work, my lad?" said he to Dick. "That I would, but I do not know how to get any," answered Dick. "If you are willing, come along with me," said the gentleman, and took him to a hay-field, where Dick worked briskly, and lived merrily till the hay was made.

After this he found himself as badly off as before; and being almost starved again, he laid himself down at the door of Mr Fitzwarren, a rich merchant. Here he was soon seen by the cook-maid, who was an ill-tempered creature, and happened just then to be very busy dressing dinner for her master and mistress; so she called out to poor Dick: "What business have you there, you lazy rogue? there is nothing else but beggars; if you do not take yourself away, we will see how you will like a sousing of some dish-water; I have some here hot enough to make you jump."

Just at that time Mr Fitzwarren himself came home to dinner; and when he saw a dirty ragged boy lying at the door, he said to him: "Why do you lie there, my boy? You seem old enough to work; I am afraid you are inclined to be lazy."

"No, indeed, sir," said Dick to him, "that is not the case, for I would work with all my heart, but I do not know anybody, and I believe I am very sick for the want of food." "Poor fellow, get up ; let me see what ails you."

Dick now tried to rise, but was obliged to lie down again, being too weak to stand, for he had not eaten any food for three days, and was no longer able to run about and beg a halfpenny of people in the street. So the kind merchant ordered him to be taken into the house, and have a good dinner given him, and be kept to do what dirty work he was able for the cook.

Little Dick would have lived very happy in this good family if it had not been for the ill-natured cook, who was finding fault and scolding him from morning to night, and besides, she was so fond of basting, that when she had no meat to baste, she would baste poor Dick's head and shoulders with a broom, or anything else that happened to fall in her way. At last her ill-usage of him was told to Alice, Mr Fitzwarren's daughter, who told the cook she should be turned away if she did not treat him kinder.

The ill-humour of the cook was now a little amended ; but besides this Dick had another hardship to get over. His bed stood in a garret, where there were so many holes in the floor and the walls that every night he was tormented with rats and mice. A gentleman having given Dick a penny for cleaning his shoes, he thought he would buy a cat with it. The next day he saw a girl with a cat, and asked her if she would let him have it for a penny. The girl said she would, and at the same time told him the cat was an excellent mouser.

Dick hid his cat in the garret, and always took care to carry a part of his dinner to her ; and in a short time he had no more trouble with the rats and mice, but slept quite sound every night.

Soon after this, his master had a ship ready to sail ; and as he thought it right that all his servants should have some chance for good fortune as well as himself, he called them all into the parlour and asked them what they would send out.

They all had something that they were willing to venture except poor Dick, who had neither money nor goods, and therefore could send nothing.

For this reason he did not come into the parlour with the rest ; but Miss Alice guessed what was the matter, and ordered him to be called in. She then said she would lay down some money for him, from her own purse ; but the father told her this would not do, for it must be something of his own.

When poor Dick heard this, he said he had nothing but a cat which he bought for a penny some time since of a little girl.

"Fetch your cat then, my good boy," said Mr Fitzwarren, " and let her go."

Dick went upstairs and brought down poor puss, with tears in his eyes, and gave her to the captain ; for he said he should now be kept awake again all night by the rats and mice.

All the company laughed at Dick's odd venture; and Miss Alice, who felt pity for the poor boy, gave him some money to buy another cat.

This, and many other marks of kindness shown him by Miss Alice, made the ill-tempered cook jealous of poor Dick, and she began to use him more cruelly than ever, and always made game of him for sending his cat to sea. She asked him if he thought his cat would sell for as much money as would buy a stick to beat him.

At last poor Dick could not bear this usage any longer, and he thought he would run away from his place; so he packed up his few things, and started very early in the morning, on All-Hallow's Day, which is the first of November. He walked as far as Holloway; and there sat down on a stone, which to this day is called Whittington's stone, and began to think to himself which road he should take as he went onwards.

While he was thinking what he should do, the Bells of Bow Church, which at that time had only six, began to ring, and he fancied their sound seemed to say to him,—

> "Turn again, Whittington,
> Lord Mayor of London."

"Lord Mayor of London!" said he to himself.

"Why, to be sure, I would put up with almost anything now, to be Lord Mayor of London, and ride in
a fine coach, when I grow to be a man! Well, I will
go back, and think nothing of the cuffing and scolding
of the old cook, if I am to be Lord Mayor of London
at last."

Dick went back, and was lucky enough to get into
the house, and set about his work, before the old cook
came downstairs.

The ship, with the cat on board, was a long time
at sea; and was at last driven by the winds on a
part of the coast of Barbary, where the only people
were the Moors, that the English had never known
before.

The people then came in great numbers to see the
sailors, who were of different colour to themselves, and
treated them very civilly; and, when they became
better acquainted, were very eager to buy the fine
things that the ship was loaded with.

When the captain saw this, he sent patterns of the
best things he had to the king of the country; who
was so much pleased with them, that he sent for the
captain to the palace. Here they were placed, as it is
the custom of the country, on rich carpets marked
with gold and silver flowers. The king and queen
were seated at the upper end of the room; and a
number of dishes were brought in for dinner. They
had not sat long, when a vast number of rats and mice
rushed in, helping themselves from almost every dish.

The captain wondered at this, and asked if these vermin were not very unpleasant.

"Oh, yes," said they, " very destructive ; and the king would give half his treasure to be freed of them, for they not only destroy his dinner, as you see, but they assault him in his chamber, and even in bed, so that he is obliged to be watched while he is sleeping for fear of them."

The captain jumped for joy ; he remembered poor Whittington and his cat, and told the king he had a creature on board the ship that would despatch all these vermin immediately. The king's heart heaved so high at the joy which this news gave him that his turban dropped off his head. "Bring this creature to me," says he ; "vermin are dreadful in a court, and if she will perform what you say, I will load your ship with gold and jewels, in exchange for her." The captain, who knew his business, took this opportunity to set forth the merits of Miss Puss. He told his majesty that it would be inconvenient to part with her, as, when she was gone, the rats and mice might destroy the goods in the ship—but to oblige his majesty he would fetch her. "Run, run!" said the queen ; "I am impatient to see the dear creature."

Away went the captain to the ship, while another dinner was got ready. He put puss under his arm, and arrived at the place soon enough to see the table full of rats.

When the cat saw them, she did not wait for

bidding, but jumped out of the captain's arms, and in a few minutes laid almost all the rats and mice dead at her feet. The rest of them in their fright scampered away to their holes.

The king and queen were quite charmed to get so easily rid of such plagues, and desired that the creature who had done them so great a kindness might be brought to them for inspection. Upon which the captain called : " Pussy, pussy, pussy ! " and she came to him. He then presented her to the queen, who started back, and was afraid to touch a creature who had made such a havoc among the rats and mice. However, when the captain stroked the cat and called : " Pussy, pussy," the queen also touched her and cried : " Putty, putty," for she had not learned English. He then put her down on the queen's lap, where she, purring, played with her majesty's hand, and then sung herself to sleep.

The king, having seen the exploits of Mrs. Puss, and being informed that her kittens would stock the whole country, bargained with the captain for the whole ship's cargo, and then gave him ten times as much for the cat as all the rest amounted to.

The captain then took leave of the royal party, and set sail with a fair wind for England, and after a happy voyage arrived safe in London.

One morning Mr Fitzwarren had just come to his counting-house and seated himself at the desk, when somebody came tap, tap, at the door. " Who's

there!" says Mr Fitzwarren. "A friend," answered
the other; "I come to bring you good news of your
ship *Unicorn*." The merchant, bustling up instantly,
opened the door, and who should be seen waiting but
the captain and factor, with a cabinet of jewels, and a
bill of lading, for which the merchant lifted up his
eyes and thanked heaven for sending him such a
prosperous voyage.

They then told the story of the cat, and showed
the rich present that the king and queen had sent for
her to poor Dick. As soon as the merchant heard
this, he called out to his servants,—

"Go fetch him—we will tell him of the same;
Pray call him Mr Whittington by name."

Mr Fitzwarren now showed himself to be a good
man; for when some of his servants said so great a
treasure was too much for Dick, he answered: "God
forbid I should deprive him of the value of a single
penny."

He then sent for Dick, who at that time was
scouring pots for the cook, and was quite dirty.

Mr Fitzwarren ordered a chair to be set for him,
and so he began to think they were making game of
him, at the same time begging them not to play tricks
with a poor simple boy, but to let him go down again,
if they pleased, to his work.

"Indeed, Mr Whittington," said the merchant,
"we are all quite in earnest with you, and I most

heartily rejoice in the news these gentlemen have brought you ; for the captain has sold your cat to the King of Barbary, and brought you in return for her more riches than I possess in the whole world ; and I wish you may long enjoy them!"

Mr Fitzwarren then told the men to open the great treasure they had brought with them ; and said : "Mr Whittington has nothing to do but to put it in some place of safety."

Poor Dick hardly knew how to behave himself for joy. He begged his master to take what part of it he pleased, since he owed it all to his kindness. "No, no," answered Mr Fitzwarren, "this is all your own ; and I have no doubt but you will use it well."

Dick next asked his mistress, and then Miss Alice, to accept a part of his good fortune ; but they would not, and at the same time told him they felt great joy at his good success. But this poor fellow was too kind-hearted to keep it all to himself ; so he made a present to the captain, the mate, and the rest of Mr Fitzwarren's servants ; and even to the ill-natured old cook.

After this Mr Fitzwarren advised him to send for a proper tradesman and get himself dressed like a gentleman ; and told him he was welcome to live in his house till he could provide himself with a better.

When Whittington s face was washed, his hair curled, his hat cocked, and he was dressed in a nice suit of clothes, he was as handsome and genteel as any

young man who visited at Mr Fitzwarren's ; so that
Miss Alice, who had once been so kind to him, and
thought of him with pity, now looked upon him as fit
to be her sweetheart ; and the more so, no doubt,
because Whittington was now always thinking what he
could do to oblige her, and making her the prettiest
presents that could be.

Mr Fitzwarren soon saw their love for each other,
and proposed to join them in marriage ; and to this
they both readily agreed. A day for the wedding was
soon fixed ; and they were attended to church by the
Lord Mayor, the court of aldermen, the sheriffs, and a
great number of the richest merchants in London,
whom they afterwards treated with a very rich feast.

History tells us that Mr Whittington and his lady
lived in great splendour, and were very happy. They
had several children. He was Sheriff of London, also
Mayor, and received the honour of knighthood by
Henry V.

The figure of Sir Richard Whittington with his
cat in his arms, carved in stone, was to be seen till the
year 1780 over the archway of the old prison of Newgate, that stood across Newgate Street.

The King of the Vipers

NEAR Norman Cross was a large lake or "mere," about whose borders tall reeds were growing, and beyond this, at a somewhat greater distance, was a wild sequestered spot surrounded with woods and thick groves, the deserted seat of some ancient family. A place more solitary and wild could scarcely be imagined ; the garden and walks were overgrown with weeds and briers, and the woods were tangled and unpruned. About this domain I would wander till overtaken by fatigue, and there I would sit down with my back against some beech, elm or stately alder tree, and, taking out my book, would pass hours in a state of unmixed enjoyment, my eyes now fixed on the wondrous pages, now glancing at the sylvan scene around ; and sometimes I would drop the book and listen to the voice of the rooks and wild pigeons, or to the croaking of multitudes of frogs from the neighbouring swamps and fens.

In going to and fro from this place I frequently passed a tall, elderly individual, dressed in rather a quaint fashion, with a skin cap on his head and stout gaiters on his legs ; on his shoulders hung a moderate sized leather sack ; he seemed fond of loitering near sunny banks, and of groping amidst furze and low scrubby bramble bushes, of which there were plenty in the neighbourhood of Norman Cross. Once I saw him standing in the middle of a dusty road, looking intently at a large mark which seemed to have been drawn across it, as if by a walking-stick.

" He must have been a large one," the old man muttered half to himself, " or he would not have left such a trail ; I wonder if he is near ; he seems to have moved this way."

He then went behind some bushes which grew on the right side of the road, and appeared to be in quest of something, moving behind the bushes with his head downwards, and occasionally striking their roots with his foot. At length he exclaimed, " Here he is ! " and I saw him dart amongst the bushes. There was a kind of scuffling noise, the rustling of branches, and the crackling of dry sticks. " I have him," said the man at last ; " I have got him ! " and presently he made his appearance about twenty yards down the road, holding a large viper in his hand. "What do you think of that, my boy ? " said he, as I went up to him ; " what do you think of catching such a thing with the naked hand ? " "What do I think ? " said I. " Why, that I could do as much myself." " You do, do you ? " said the man ; and opening his bag he thrust the reptile into it, which was far from empty.

As I was returning, towards the evening, I overtook the old man, who was wending in the same direction. " Good evening to you, sir," said I, taking off my cap. " Good evening," said the old man ; and then looking at me, " How's this ? " said he, " you aren't, sure, the child I met in the morning ? Why, you were then all froth and conceit, and now you take off your cap to me." " I beg your pardon," said I, "if I was frothy and conceited : it ill becomes a child like me to be so." " That's true, dear," said the old man ; " well, as you have begged my pardon, I truly forgive you." " Thank you," said I ; " have you caught many more of those things ? " " Only four or five," said the old man ; " they are getting scarce, though this used to be a great neighbourhood for them. I hunt them mostly for the fat they contain, which is good for various sore troubles, especially for the rheumatism." " And do you get your living by hunting these creatures?" I demanded. "Not altogether," said the old man. "I am what they call a herbalist, one who knows the virtue of particular herbs; I gather them at the proper season to make medicines for the sick, but I do not live in this neighbourhood in particular, I travel about; I have not been here for many years."

.   .   .   .

From this time the old man and myself formed an acquaintance; I often accompanied him in his wanderings about the neighbourhood, and on two or three occasions assisted him in catching the reptiles which he hunted. He was fond of telling me anecdotes connected with his adventures with reptiles. "But," said he one day, sighing, "I must shortly give up this business, I am no longer the man I was, I am become timid, and when a person is timid in viper-hunting he had better leave off, as it is clear his virtue is forsaking him. I got a fright some years ago, which I am sure I shall never get the better of; my hand has been shaky more or less ever since." "What frightened you?" I asked. "I had better not tell you," said the old man, "or you may be frightened too, lose your virtue, and be no longer good for the business." "I don't care," said I; "I don't intend to follow the business: I daresay I shall be an officer, like my father." "Well," said the old man, "I once saw the king of the vipers, and since then—" "The king of the vipers!" said I, interrupting him, "have the vipers

a king?"   "As sure as we have," said the old man,
"as sure as we have King George to rule over us, have
these reptiles a king to rule over them."   "And where
did you see him?" said I.   "I will tell you," said the
old man, "though I don't like talking about the matter.
About seven years ago I happened to be far down
yonder to the west, on the other side of England.   It
was a very sultry day, about three o'clock in the afternoon, when I found myself on some heathy land near
the sea, on the ridge of a hill, the side of which, nearly
as far down as the sea, was heath ; but on the top there
was ground which had been planted, and from which
the harvest had been gathered—oats or barley, I know
not which—but I remember that the ground was
covered with stubble.   Well, from the heat of the day
and from having walked about for hours, I felt very
tired ; so I laid myself down, my head just on the
ridge of the hill, towards the field, and my body over
the side down amongst the heath.   My bag, which was
nearly filled with creatures, lay at a little distance from
my face ;   the creatures were struggling in it, I
remember, and I thought to myself, how much more
comfortably off I was than they ;   I was taking my ease
on the nice open hill, cooled by the breezes, whilst they
were in the nasty close bag, coiling about one another,
and breaking their very hearts.   Little by little I closed
my eyes, and fell into the sweetest snooze ; and there I
lay over the hill's side, I don't know how long.   At
last it seemed to me that I heard a noise in my sleep,

something like a thing moving, very faint, however, far away ; then it died, and then it came again upon my ear as I slept, and now it appeared almost as if I heard crackle, crackle ; then it died again, or I became yet more dead asleep than before, I know not which, but I certainly lay some time without hearing it. All of a sudden I became awake, and there was I, on the ridge of the hill, with my cheek on the ground towards the stubble, with a noise in my ear like that of something moving towards me, among the stubble of the field ; well, I lay a moment or two, listening to the noise, and then I became frightened, for I did not like the noise at all, it sounded so odd ; so I rolled myself over, and looked towards the stubble.   Mercy upon us ! there was a huge snake, or rather a dreadful viper, for it was all yellow and gold, moving towards me, bearing its head about a foot and a half above the ground, the dry stubble crackling beneath it.   It might be about five yards off when I first saw it, making straight towards me, child, as if it would devour me.   I lay quite still, for I was stupefied with horror, whilst the creature came still nearer ; and now it was nearly upon me, when it suddenly drew back a little, and then—what do you think ?—it lifted its head and chest high in the air, and high over my face as I looked up, flickering at me with its tongue as if it would fly at my face. Child, what I felt at that moment I can scarcely say, but it was a sufficient punishment for all the sins I ever committed : and there we two were, I looking up at the viper, and the viper looking down upon me, flickering at me with its tongue. It was only the kindness of God that saved me : all at once there was a loud noise, the report of a gun, for a fowler was shooting at some birds, a little way off in the stubble. Whereupon the viper sunk its head and immediately made off over the ridge of the hill, down in the direction of the sea. As it passed by me, however—and it passed close by me—it hesitated a moment, as if it was doubtful whether it should not seize me ; it did not, however, but made off down the hill. It has often struck me that he was angry with me, and came upon me unawares for presuming to meddle with his people, as I have always been in the habit of doing."

"But," said I, "how do you know that it was the king of the vipers ?"

"How do I know ?" said the old man, "who else should it be? There was as much difference between it and other reptiles as between King George and other people."

THE KING OF THE CATS

ONCE upon a time there were two brothers who lived in a lonely house in a very lonely part of Scotland ; an old woman used to do the cooking, and there was no one else, unless we count her cat and their own dogs, within miles of them.

One autumn afternoon the elder of the two, whom we will call Elshender, said he would not go out, so the younger one, Fergus, went alone to follow the path where they had been shooting the day before, far across the mountains. He meant to return home before the early sunset ; however, he did not do so, and Elshender became very uneasy as he watched and waited in vain till long after their usual supper-time. At last Fergus returned, wet and exhausted, nor did he explain why he was so late.

But after supper when the two brothers were seated before the fire, on which the peat crackled cheerfully, the dogs lying at their feet, and the old woman's black cat sitting gravely with half-shut eyes on the hearth between them, Fergus recovered himself and began to tell his adventures.

"You must be wondering," said he, "what made me so late ? I have had a very, very strange

My stars! Old Peter's dead and I'm the King o' the Cats!

adventure to-day ; I hardly know what to say about it. I went, as I told you I should, along our yesterday's track ; a mountain fog came on just as I was about to turn homewards, and I completely lost my way. I wandered about for a long time not knowing where I was, till at last I saw a light, and made for it, hoping to get help. As I came near it, it disappeared, and I found myself close to an old oak tree. I climbed into the branches the better to look for the light, and, behold ! there it was right beneath me, inside the hollow trunk of the tree. I seemed to be looking down into a church, where a funeral was taking place. I heard singing, and saw a coffin surrounded by torches, all carried by— But I know you won't believe me, Elshender, if I tell you ! "

His brother eagerly begged him to go on, and threw a dry peat on the fire to encourage him. The dogs were sleeping quietly, but the cat was sitting up and seemed to be listening just as carefully and cannily as Elshender himself. Both brothers indeed turned their eyes on the cat as Fergus took up his story.

" Yes," he continued, " it is as true as I sit here. The coffin and the torches were both carried by cats, and upon the coffin were marked a crown and a sceptre ! "

He got no further, for the black cat started up shrieking : " My stars ! old Peter's dead, and I'm the King o' the Cats ! "—then rushed up the chimney and was seen no more.

CHICKEN LICKEN

**A**S Chicken-licken went one day to the wood, an acorn fell upon her poor bald pate, and she thought the sky had fallen. So she said she would go and tell the King the sky had fallen. So Chicken-licken turned back, and met Hen-len. "Well, Hen-len,

where are you going?" And Hen-len said, "I'm
going to the wood for some meat." And Chicken-
licken said, "Oh! Hen-len, don't go, for I was going,
and the sky fell upon my poor bald pate, and I'm going
to tell the King." So Hen-len turned back with
Chicken-licken, and met Cock-lock. "Oh! Cock-
lock, where are you going?" And Cock-lock said,
"I'm going to the wood for some meat." Then Hen-
len said, "Oh! Cock-lock, don't go, for I was going,
and I met Chicken-licken, and Chicken-licken had
been at the wood, and the sky had fallen on her poor
bald pate, and we are going to tell the King."

So Cock-lock turned back, and met Duck-luck.
"Well, Duck-luck, where are you going?" And
Duck-luck said, "I'm going to the wood for some
meat." Then Cock-lock said, "Oh! Duck-luck, don't
go, for I was going, and I met Hen-len, and Hen-len
met Chicken-licken, and Chicken-licken had been at
the wood, and the sky had fallen on her poor bald
pate, and we are going to tell the King."

So Duck-luck turned back, and met Drake-lake.
"Well, Drake-lake, where are you going?" And Drake-
lake said, "I'm going to the wood for some meat."
Then Duck-luck said, "Oh! Drake-lake, don't go, for
I was going, and I met Cock-lock, and Cock-lock met
Hen-len, and Hen-len met Chicken-licken, and Chicken-
licken had been at the wood, and the sky had fallen on
her poor bald pate, and we are going to tell the King."

So Drake-lake turned back, and met Goose-loose.

"Well, Goose-loose, where are you going?" And Goose-loose said, "I'm going to the wood for some meat." Then Drake-lake said, "Oh! Goose-loose, don't go, for I was going, and I met Duck-luck, and Duck-luck met Cock-lock, and Cock-lock met Hen-len, and Hen-len met Chicken-licken, and Chicken-licken had been at the wood, and the sky had fallen on her poor bald pate, and we are going to tell the King."

So Goose-loose turned back, and met Gander-lander. "Well, Gander-lander, where are you going?" And Gander-lander said, "I'm going to the wood for some meat." Then Goose-loose said, "Oh! Gander-lander, don't go, for I was going, and I met Drake-lake, and Drake-lake met Duck-luck, and Duck-luck met Cock-lock, and Cock-lock met Hen-len, and Hen-len met Chicken-licken, and Chicken-licken had been at the wood, and the sky had fallen on her poor bald pate, and we are going to tell the King."

So Gander-lander turned back, and met Turkey-lurkey. "Well, Turkey-lurkey, where are you going?" And Turkey-lurkey said, "I'm going to the wood for some meat." Then Gander-lander said, "Oh! Turkey-lurkey, don't go, for I was going, and I met Goose-loose, and Goose-loose met Drake-lake, and Drake-lake met Duck-luck, and Duck-luck met Cock-lock, and Cock-lock met Hen-len, and Hen-len met Chicken-licken, and Chicken-licken had been at the wood, and the sky had fallen on her poor bald pate, and we are going to tell the King."

So Turkey-lurkey turned back, and walked with Gander-lander, Goose-loose, Drake-lake, Duck-luck, Cock-lock, Hen-len, and Chicken-licken. And as they were going along, they met Fox-lox. And Fox-lox said, "Where are you going, my pretty maids?" And they said, "Chicken-licken went to the wood, and the sky fell upon her poor bald pate, and we are going to tell the King." And Fox-lox said, "Come along with me, and I will show you the way." But Fox-lox took them into the fox's hole, and he and his young ones soon ate up poor Chicken-licken, Hen-len, Cock-lock, Duck-luck, Drake-lake, Goose-loose, Gander-lander, and Turkey-lurkey, and they never saw the King to tell him that the sky had fallen.

H. C

QUEEN MAB'S BED

UPON six plump dandelions, high-
Reared, lies her elvish majesty,
Whose woolly bubbles seemed to drown
Her Mabship in obedient down ;
And next to these, two blankets o'er-
Cast of the finest gossamer ;
And then a rug of carded wool,
Which, sponge-like, drinking in the dull
Light of the moon, seemed to comply,[1]
Cloud-like, the dainty deity.
Thus soft she lies ; and over-head
A spinner's[2] circle is bespread
With cobweb curtains, from the roof
So neatly sunk, as that no proof
Of any tackling can declare
What gives it hanging in the air.
And now sleeps Mab : out goes the light ;
I wish both her and thee good-night.

[1] Enfold.   [2] Spider's.